MAD WITH MUCH HEART

A child has been killed and the village scours the snowy countryside for the murderer. Bond takes it personal when the fiend makes an attempt on his own daughter's life, and swears to kill him. It's up to James Wilson, the big city cop, to try to instill some order and sanity to the hunt. But then the killer is spotted, and the chase is on.

Wilson and Bond grab a car and take off after him—Bond half-crazed with vengeance, Wilson just trying to catch up to the man in the snow. Then their car plows into a snowbank, and it becomes a foot chase. That's when they come to the farmhouse. Inside is a young woman named Mary. It takes them both awhile to realize that she's blind. But more than that, Mary is holding a secret, one that will change *all* their lives.

"Butler does a very nice job conveying the physical effort of running and driving through deep snow, the slippery suspense of a slow-motion car-chase over icy country lanes, and the sheer exhaustion of mind and body brought on by the cold... the visceral quality of the story and his prose keeps one turning the pages."
—Dan Stumpf, *Mystery*File*

Gerald Butler Bibliography
(1907-1988)

Novels:
Kiss the Blood Off My Hands (1940; reprinted in U.S.
  as *The Unafraid*, 1948)
They Cracked Her Glass Slipper (1941)
Their Rainbow Had Black Edges (1943; reprinted in U.S.
  as *Dark Rainbow*, 1945)
Mad With Much Heart (1945; reprinted in U.S.
  as *The Lurking Man*, 1952)
Slippery Hitch (1946)
Blow Hot, Blow Cold (1951; reprinted in U.S.
  as *Choice of Two Women*, 1960)
There Is a Death, Elizabeth (1972)

MAD WITH MUCH HEART

GERALD BUTLER

Introduction by Curtis Evans

Stark House Press • Eureka California

MAD WITH MUCH HEART

Published by Stark House Press
1315 H Street
Eureka, CA 95501, USA
griffinskye3@sbcglobal.net
www.starkhousepress.com

MAD WITH MUCH HEART
Originally published by Jarrolds Publishing, London, 1945; and Farrar &
Rinehart, Inc. New York, 1946; copyright © 1946 by Gerald Butler.
Reprinted in paperback by Lion Books, New York, 1952, as *The Lurking
Man*.

ISBN: 979-8-88601-125-8

Cover & Text design by Mark Shepard, shepgraphics.com
Proofreading by Bill Kelly

First Stark House Press Edition: February 2025

7
Mad with Much Heart (1945),
Gerald Butler
By Curtis Evans

11
Mad With Much Heart
By Gerald Butler

Mad with Much Heart (1945), Gerald Butler

By Curtis Evans

> —Fill'd with her love, may I be rather grown
> Mad with much heart, than idiot with none.
> —John Donne, "Elegy X"

1946 was a banner year in the United States for English novelist Gerald Butler, the kind of year that writers dream about. In England between 1940 and 1945 Butler had published three novels—successively the evocatively-titled *Kiss the Blood off My Hands* (1940), *Their Rainbows Had Black Edges* (1943) and *Mad with Much Heart* (1945). When the Englishman finally was picked up for American publication in 1945—see my introduction to Stark House's edition of *Kiss the Blood off My Hands* for that unusual story—*Rainbows* was published at the end of year, with much of its poetic title shorn, as *Dark Rainbow*. The next year Butler's James M. Cainish melodrama *Kiss the Bood off My Hands* was published to much success and a promising film deal, resulting in the author's publisher, Rinehart, hustling to get the next Butler title out for eager purchasers before Christmas. This was *Mad with Much Heart*, which had just appeared in England the previous year.

With *Mad with Much Heart* Butler further heightened the narrative minimalism of *Kiss the Blood off My Hands*, such that the plot can be sufficiently summarized in a few sentences. A mad killer has run amok during a bleak midwinter in rural Yorkshire, slaying one girl and attacking another, who survived. The local inhabitants are in a frenzy, especially Farmer Bond, whose own daughter was the second attack victim. He has personally vowed to pursue and put an end to the murderer with his own hands. Into the area comes a hardened London policeman, James Wilson, tasked with carrying out the commission of the law. He is determined that his quarry shall be taken alive. Eventually the two men, cop and farmer, chase the killer across the countryside, coming upon the isolated, snowbound cottage of Mary Maldon, a beautiful, young blind woman who seems to know more about the matter at hand than she cares to admit....

Like *Kiss the Blood off My Hands, Mad with Much Heart* scored with American book reviewers. Proclaimed Ralph M. Williams in the *Chicago Tribune*: "Few writers can convey complex moves and motives in such simple, forceful English as does Gerald Butler." In the *Macon News* Joe Parham compared Butler's "mystery thriller" for sheer suspense to the works of Cornell Woolrich and "acknowledged master" Alfred Hitchcock. In the *Montgomery Advertiser* Ray Gould—who had previously raved about *Kiss the Blood off My Hands*—deemed *Heart* even better than *Blood*, declaring that: "It is potent stuff, a turbulent drama with thrills, suspense, excitement, and strange romance.... Gerald Butler proves himself an unusual writer of breathtaking realism [and adds] a sympathy and tenderness not shown before in his two books published in this country." Joseph E. English in the *Springfield Daily Republican* avowed that Butler's new novel "is as tense and fast moving a book as any mystery fan could desire. Once the first page has been completed, the reader has no respite until the book has been closed."

While *Heart* like *Blood* can simply be read as a crime thriller melodrama, both novels in fact are concerned with the same central theme (which many critics seemed to miss in *Blood*): the uplifting impact of empathy, as embodied in the love of a man for a woman, on even the most embittered of human souls. As the title suggests, we are better off mad with much heart than idiots with none. It is a lesson Wilson has yet to learn when he first appears in the novel. "I think I hate London really," he confides to country girl Mary. "In my job I only see the rotten side of it."

Later he thinks to himself about his bad experiences with crooks and conning women: "There was never anything clear and clean, never any gift without a hook in it, never any meeting without some undercover deceit.... Knowing that, it made you hate them, and it gradually made you think they were all the same.... gradually it came eating into you, and you couldn't meet anyone fair and square somehow."

This theme likely is what appealed to director Nicholas Ray, director of the film version of *Mad with Much Heart*, which was released under the title *On Dangerous Ground* in 1951. Ray, known for the classic noirs *They Live by Night* and *In a Lonely Place*, the bizarre color western noir *Johnny Guitar* and the angsty teenage melodrama *Rebel without a Cause* (for which he received an Oscar scripting nomination), obviously saw emotional possibilities in *Mad with Much Heart* and he splendidly realized them in *On Dangerous Ground*.

Location shooting on the film, which was produced by John Houseman and starred Robert Ryan as James Wilson and Ida Lupino as Mary Maldon, took place during a relentlessly hanging-on winter in March 1950 at Granby, Colorado, a little Rocky Mountains village buffeted by high winds and below freezing temperatures. After just the first day of filming, the crewmen were all suffering from painfully chapped faces, in contrast with the visages of the greasepainted cast, which remained in excellent repair. There being no cold cream left on the barely stocked shelves in Granby, the burly crew gritted their chattering teeth and donned the actors' makeup, much to the amusement of the locals.

This comical anecdote notwithstanding, *On Dangerous Ground* is an exceptionally serious film. The screenplay, by Ray and A. I. Bezzerides, who is best known today for having scripted the hard-boiled classic *Kiss Me Deadly* (freely adapted from the Mickey Spillane novel), considerably expands the plot of *Mad with Much Heart*, providing what essentially is a thirty-minute prologue illustrating Wilson's words from the novel about the city corroding a cop like acid, so that "you couldn't meet anyone fair and square somehow." It is a powerful story in its own right, with strong performances by Ryan as a violently angry, near-psychotic cop and by a range of effectively cast supporting players, including Charles Kemper as Wilson's cop pal who gives him a needed telling off (his last performance), Richard Irving as sleazy hood Bernie, Cleo Moore as masochistic moll Myrna and Nita Talbot, likely familiar to people of the Baby Boom and Gen X generations for her Sixties and Seventies television series guest parts, in a cameo as one sultry piece of blonde bar jailbait.

The remaining fifty minutes of *Ground* sees Wilson sent up north literally to "cool off" by investigating a local murder. (Presumably the film is set in New York City and somewhere in the Adirondacks upstate, though there had been talk of placing the flick in Boston and the Berkshires.) The rest of the story pretty closely follows the book narrative, with Ida Lupino, Ward Bond and young Sumner

Williams, the director's own nephew, effectively embodying the characters of Mary, Bond and Danny (though Bond's surname, which he coincidently shared with the actor playing him, is changed to Brent).

Upon its release *Ground* received largely mixed to negative notices, with many reviewers complaining about what Ernie Schier in the Washington, D. C. *Times Herald* called a "jigsaw puzzle with too many pieces missing." Like a lot of other reviewers, Schier did not believe that the two-part structure of the film really fitted together. On the other hand, Jay Carmody of the rival *Washington Examiner*, found the film a "neatly blended" melodrama. Since the 1990s critics have increasingly lauded the film as one of Nicholas Ray's most distinguished works. If *On Dangerous Ground* is only semi-noir, it does move the heart—that, I think, safely can be said.

—November 2024

· ·

Curtis Evans received a PhD in American history in 1998. He is the author of *Masters of the "Humdrum" Mystery: Cecil John Charles Street, Freeman Wills Crofts, Alfred Walter Stewart and British Detective Fiction, 1920-1961* (2012), *Clues and Corpses: The Detective Fiction and Mystery Criticism of Todd Downing* (2013), *The Spectrum of English Murder: The Detective Fiction of Henry Lancelot Aubrey-Fletcher and G. D. H. and Margaret Cole* (2015) and editor of the Edgar nominated *Murder in the Closet: Essays on Queer Clues in Crime Fiction Before Stonewall* (2017). He writes about vintage crime fiction at his blog The Passing Tramp and at Crimereads.

MAD WITH MUCH HEART

GERALD BUTLER

"may I be rather grown
Mad with much heart, than idiot with none."

ONE

It was after seven when he reached the farmhouse, and it had been quite dark for the last two hours. He fumbled with the handle of the front door, but when he had turned the handle, the door would not yield to his pressure. He kicked his foot against it, hard, with the sudden irritation of a man who finds his own door locked against him. From inside the door he heard footsteps coming along the stone floor of the hallway, and then he heard her voice calling:

"Who is there?"

"It's me," he answered irritably. "Open the door." It annoyed him to find his own door barred against him, even though he knew the reason. But the annoyance quickly went as he heard the bolt being hurriedly pulled back. He knew that it was wiser that way. He knew that throughout the whole village, and all the villages around, there would not be a single door left unbarred that night.

Now his door was pulled open, and he stepped across the mat into the hall. The icy cold air from outside came stabbing into the hall like a sharp knife, and his wife pushed quickly past him to slam the door against that biting cold. She slid the heavy bolt again, and then turned to follow her husband into the parlour. He walked slowly, wearily, and just from looking at the back of his shoulders and seeing the melancholy droop of his arms, she knew what the answer was, she knew that he had nothing to tell her. He propped his double-barrelled shotgun against the wall by the side of the fireplace, and then stood in front of the fire, working his fingers to coax the warmth back into them. His wife bent down and lifted the kettle from the hob, and poured the boiling water into a teapot that was standing ready with the tea inside it. She waited a couple of minutes for the tea to brew. Neither of them spoke. Then she poured a cup of the dark, strong tea and held it out to him. He took it and started to sip it slowly. She stood there waiting for him to speak, but he gave no sign of intending to. She knew the answer, but she had to ask.

"You didn't find anything?"

He finished drinking the tea in silence. Then he shook his head slowly.

"Not a trace of anything," he said. "The whole countryside has been searching, but there's not a trace of anything. The cold's against us. The cold is on his side. The ground is frozen so hard that you couldn't leave a footprint if you tried."

"What are the police doing?" she asked. "Can't the police do something?"

"Nobody can do anything until they've found the man who did it."

"But you may not find him," she said. "What will happen if you don't find him?"

The man pressed his teeth together and then pressed his lips together, and his eyes went hard like bits of highly polished stone.

"We shall find him," he said. "There's not a man for miles round that'll stop searching until we have found him. And when we've found him"—he spoke very coldly and deliberately—"when we've found him we shall kill him, we shall kill him slowly, bit by bit, tearing him to pieces with our hands."

His wife was looking at him, and she felt a little shiver go through her as she heard him speaking. It frightened her, more than she was frightened already, to hear him speak like that. She put out her hand and touched his arm.

"Walter," she said. She did not know quite what to say.

"Bennett was out on the search himself," he said.

"Did you speak to him?"

He shook his head. "Nobody knew what to say to him. Nobody liked to speak to him at all, somehow. He looked so terrible. He looked more like a ghost than a man. An awful look in his eyes. A terrible look."

She nodded her head slowly, understandingly.

"It's a wonder he could bear to be out with you on the search," she said. "He must be feeling as if the whole world had suddenly come to an end. Poor Mrs. Bennett—she's half crazed. That district nurse has been with her most of the day. Poor woman keeps screaming and then fainting right off. Doctor Adams has been there twice already, and done all he can. He's going again to-night. I expect he'll give her something to make her get a bit of sleep."

The man put this cup down on the edge of the table, and turned to stir the fire. The grate was heaped with blazing coals, but even into that tightly sealed room the bitter cold came creeping. He jabbed the iron poker into the glowing red heart of the fire. He jabbed it viciously and hard. When he pulled it out again the end of the poker itself was glowing red, a sullen and threatening red, and as he looked at it, his grip on the handle tightened, and he lifted the glowing poker as if it were a weapon in his hand. She watched him. She saw his knuckles grow gradually white as his grip grew fiercer. She saw his eyes go cold and distant, as if he were seeing beyond the room and out across the frozen fields. She was frightened by the look of him, and she wanted to put out her hand and touch his arm again, to soften him, to soothe him. But the searing hot poker was in his hands, and she did not like to move.

His eyes came gradually back into the room, and the tension slackened in him. The end of the poker was black again now, and he dropped it on to the stone of the hearth. Then he spoke as if he thought he were alone in the room.

"Why are such things allowed to happen?" he asked. "Has the eye of the Lord left our village?"

She shuddered a little as she heard him.

"Walter," she said. "Please don't talk like that. That is a blasphemy."

He shook his head slowly.

"No," he said. "Out in the field there—that is the blasphemy. That is the thing that must not go unpunished."

His voice was even and calm again now, and she went to him, reaching for one of his hands and holding it in hers, just for the sake of touching him, for the sake of feeling the real flesh and blood and companionship of him. And he sensed the need in her, and he put his other arm round her shoulders, holding her firmly.

"I wish you hadn't seen it, old girl," he said kindly. "You must try to forget it. You must try hard all the time to think of other things."

The sudden softening of his voice knocked the props from under her. While he had been taut and fierce, she had been held tight by the tension of him. Now the nerves inside her slackened and sagged, and she put her head on his shoulder and cried quietly.

"It's not like someone dying," she whispered, sobbingly. "It's like— it's like . . . you couldn't even feel that her little soul had gone to rest in peace. Her face was still in torment . . ."

The man gripped her tighter, and gave her a little shake.

"Don't, Ellen," he said. "Don't think back to it. Try to forget that you saw it at all. Don't let your mind hold the picture of it. When it tries to come into your mind, push it away. Push it away!"

She shook her head helplessly.

"I'm trying all the time, but it keeps coming back. It was their only one, too. I remember when that little Betty came into the world. Doctor Adams brought her. They thought Mrs. Bennett was going to die. And afterwards, when they let me go and see her, she said she would willingly have gone through twice as much for such a lovely baby. She had wanted it so long. And now . . ." her voice broke upwards into a scream, ". . . now that only little girl of hers is just a maimed and twisted body . . ."

He shook her violently now, to stop her speaking, to stop her thinking.

"Pull yourself together!" he said, deliberately rough with her. And then: "What about supper? Aren't I going to eat any supper to-night? It's cold enough without having an empty stomach!"

She muttered something and hurried to the stove. As he watched her, the look on his face did not tally with the gruffness of his words. For a moment he almost smiled at the way it had worked. When a woman gets like that, he was thinking, you've got to give her something to do.

As they sat at their supper, they tried to talk of other things. But their thoughts were not on what they were saying, and they gradually lapsed into silence, and then gave up the effort and came back to the things that were filling their minds.

"They've sent a special policeman down from London," he said. "Chap in ordinary clothes. A detective I suppose he would call himself."

"Do you think he will catch the man?"

"We shall catch him. We don't need any fancy detectives. We shall search every ditch and every hedge and every blade of grass until we've caught him. The men have all sworn it. This policeman chap is wasting his time."

"I suppose he is looking for clues?"

"He's looking for trouble himself by the way he's going on. I've seen him. He was down at the Cricketers this evening. He was asking questions of everybody he could find. Daft questions. What we've got to do is find the man who did it. What good are a lot of daft questions going to do? The way this chap goes on, you'd think he suspected that one of the men in the village had done it. He's asking for trouble if he's not very careful. He even started asking questions of poor Bennett himself. Where was Bennett the day before? What time did Bennett go to bed the night before?" He scowled as he remembered it. "Does he think Bennett murdered his own little girl, or something? Poor Bennett could hardly answer him. The men didn't like it. They told the chap to shut up. They told it like they meant it. But five minutes later he was pestering someone else with questions."

"I suppose they have to find out all they can," she said.

"This is our own business," he said. "We didn't ask for any fancy detectives. We shall catch him. The men have sworn it. We don't need detectives trying to make us suspect each other."

She shook her head, agreeing with him.

"No," she said. "Enough evil has come to us already."

"And if this detective happens to be around when we catch the murderer," he went on, "does he think he is going to be allowed to arrest him and take him away quietly? If that is what he thinks, he is mistaken. When we catch the man, we kill the man. The men have sworn that too."

That new, unfamiliar, bloodless quality had come into his voice again. She felt that some part of him had suddenly become a stranger to her. This part that she had not seen till now was queerly frightening. As she sat and looked at him, hearing his voice, she felt as if the ice-cold air was coming into the room and blowing on her spine.

"The law must take its course," she said.

"What?" he demanded, suddenly curt, as if he were daring her to challenge this direction of his thoughts.

"I said the law must take its course," she repeated simply.

He faced her, frowning sternly.

"What kind of talking is that?" he asked her.

She looked at him, a little bewildered, uncertain how to answer him. She could not grapple with this mystifying feeling of suddenly not knowing him so well.

"What kind of talking?" She repeated his words, defensively.

His eyes were hard and the set of his mouth was hard. "Do you speak for this detective against me?"

She shook her head quickly.

"Of course not, Walter."

"Then why did you say that?"

She did not answer. She did not clearly understand what was happening.

"Why did you say that?" he pressed.

"Say what? I didn't say anything."

"You said the law must take its course."

She was silent. She wished the cold air would stop blowing against her spine.

"You were speaking against me," he said. "You were speaking for this detective."

"But Walter . . ."

"I said we have sworn to kill the man. I have sworn to kill the man."

She nodded. She felt as if she had no power to stop herself from nodding.

"So you speak against me if you say the law must take its course."

She nodded again. His voice seemed to come to her from farther and farther away.

"The law is in the hands of the first one who finds the murderer," he said.

She started to nod her head again, but she suddenly managed to take hold of herself.

"No!" she said. "No, Walter. You do not mean what you are saying. No man may take the law into his own hands."

"We have sworn it."

"No. That is adding evil to evil."

"It is merely making sure of retribution."

"The law will bring retribution. That is what the law is for."

"We do not trust the law," he said. "The law listens to excuses. Sometimes the law fails. Sometimes the law does not exact the full penalty. When we catch this man, we have sworn not to trust him to the law."

"But the law is just, Walter. The law punishes those who should be punished."

He shook his head.

"We were talking to-night," he said. "Some of the men had read in the papers only last week about a man who had done just such a thing as this. The law said that the evidence was not enough." He made a noise like spitting. "We do not trust the law."

"You must trust it, Walter."

"The law listens to excuses." His voice suddenly became thick and throaty. "Did this fiend listen for Bennett's kid to make excuses?"

"You must trust the law."

"If this detective catches the man, we'll never allow him to take him away alive."

"Thou shalt not kill, Walter."

"The men have sworn it, and I have sworn it with them."

"You do not mean what you are saying, Walter. You do not know what you are saying."

He was looking through her and beyond her. "Vengeance is mine," he said again.

"That was our Lord, Walter." Her voice was nothing but a whisper. The chill on her spine was taking her voice away.

"Vengeance is mine," he said again.

She stood up, her eyes fixed on to him. She walked slowly, backwards, towards the door. He was looking straight at her, but he did not see her and he did not know that she had gone out of the room.

She walked slowly across the hall and up the stairway. Outside a door at the top of the stairs, she paused quietly, listening. She turned the handle, inch by inch, trying to make no sound. When the latch was right back, she pushed the door open carefully, and walked on tiptoe into the room. She did not need to turn the light on, for the curtains were drawn aside and the moon had now come up and was flooding the room with pale light. She stood for several minutes looking at the bed, at the little mound of sheets and blankets that rose and fell steadily with her daughter's breathing, and the tousled ginger curls that were half buried in the pillow. As she stood and looked, she found herself praying. She did not know exactly who or what her prayer was for. It was just that the thoughts in her mind made her feel lonely, powerless, and she wanted the company of prayer. Her praying swept swiftly from the room where she was standing, downstairs to her husband, out across the field to the little murdered girl, to the empty-hearted mother and father, and back to the bundle of ginger curls as they moved slightly in sleep. Then she went softly over to the window, to check once more that the catch was securely fastened. She did not touch her daughter, for fear of waking her, but instead she moved her own lips in a kiss as she stood there. Then she went out of the door and closed it quietly behind her, and went across the landing into her own bedroom.

She undressed slowly, in the moonlight. Her mind was so full that she no longer felt the cold. She stood in her nightdress, looking out through the window, at the leafless trees and the frozen fields. In that ghostly light, the world outside looked unreal and sinister. She got into bed, and lay there listening. She lay awake for a long time, until at last she heard her husband coming up the stairs. She heard him pause at the top of the stairs as she had done. She heard him, in his turn, open their Dorothy's door and creep into the room. And then he was coming into their room, and as he came, she turned on to her side and pretended to be asleep.

Dorothy Bond's ginger curls were almost hidden by the woolly hood that her mother had put on her head to keep the cold out of her ears. She looked out of the window of the farmhouse, and saw Miss Rutter there. Miss Rutter had already collected twenty girls. The Bonds' farmhouse was the last house between the village and the school, so Dorothy was the last one to be collected. Dorothy thought that was a very nice arrangement, because already it was twenty minutes after the time when lessons were supposed to start, and Miss Rutter would not be able to tell her off for being late, because she was only late through waiting for Miss Rutter. This was the first morning of the girls being collected by Miss Rutter. Dorothy hoped the idea would continue. Miss Rutter was hoping exactly the opposite. She had been up half an hour earlier than usual, in order to go round calling for the girls, and she was now thoroughly chilled. She did not see why it was her job to do it. She agreed, of course, that the girls could not be allowed to go to school without a grown-up in charge of them. The villagers had all decided that in view of what had happened the children could not go to school without a guardian. Miss Rutter had fondly imagined that the mothers would take it in turns to shepherd the children. She did not see why it was her job.

Dorothy ran down the path. She thought it might be fun. Outside the school, opportunities seemed to present themselves for teasing teacher which never existed inside the classroom. It might be fun. They would be able to plan ways of making Miss Rutter simply furious, with the defence that they were not actually in school and so could do what they liked.

But Miss Rutter was perishingly cold, and she was not feeling in any out-of-school mood. She formed the girls up into a crocodile, two abreast. She brought up the rear. Dorothy, the last addition, was tacked on at the front. A very bad tactical position, Dorothy reflected; the teacher should have been in front, and the ringleader at the back.

The crocodile set off along the lane. The school, for some reason which no one had ever discovered, had been built right outside the village, and they had over half a mile to go. Their breath condensed in the frosty air, and for a few moments Dorothy was content to play at breathing smoke. But the others had already tired of that, and it wasn't fun for long. Then Dorothy started to make full use of the only advantage of being in front. By suddenly standing still without warning, she made the girls behind all bump into each other. This was quickly appreciated. At the second attempt, the girls got the hang of the idea and all crowded forward on top of each other in exaggerated chaos, with cries of surprise and confusion. Miss Rutter allowed it to happen twice without appearing to notice. She always believed in trying that technique first, in the hope that they would not trouble to go on doing it if they found that it did not annoy her.

But Dorothy's third sudden stop was even more drastically successful than the second. Miss Rutter called sharply.

"Dorothy Bond, walk along properly!"

"I'm sorry, Miss Rutter. I forgot there was anyone behind me."

They set off again, Dorothy now setting the style with an exaggerated stately goose-step, quickly copied by the rest. They came to a change in the surface of the road, where the rough surface finished and a smooth macadam started. And here the road was slippery with the frost. Dorothy noted this fact with delight. It was almost too good to be true. She sat down abruptly. The others piled happily on top of her.

"Dorothy!" The reprimanding voice was answered by a chorus this time.

"Dorothy slipped, Miss Rutter."

"She might easily have hurt herself, Miss Rutter."

"It's very slippery, Miss Rutter."

"Mind *you* don't slip, Miss Rutter."

"Oo! Miss Rutter—do mind you don't slip."

"If Dorothy slipped, *you* might slip, Miss Rutter."

"It's very slippery, Miss Rutter. Anybody might slip when it's slippery."

"Do *mind*, Miss Rutter."

"Everybody look out that Miss Rutter doesn't slip!"

"Some of us had better go behind you, Miss Rutter, in case you slip. If you slipped when you were at the back, then we might go on without even knowing that you'd hurt yourself."

"Everybody look out that Miss Rutter doesn't hurt herself."

"Can you stand all right, Miss Rutter?"

Miss Rutter was standing quite all right. She was waiting with all her professional patience. She stood there and waited, controlled but frozen, until the shouts gradually petered out.

"And now," she said at length, "are we ready to go on?"

The crocodile proceeded. The road was not as slippery as it looked. In fact, Dorothy joyfully told herself, it wasn't slippery at all, and it had been quite a brainwave to pretend to slip.

"I bet the pond's frozen," she said quietly to the girl who was walking beside her at the front of the column. "Coo—I bet it is!"

"How about dashing on ahead and making a slide?"

"But we can't, Dorothy. Old Rutter-Butter would be ever so cross."

"But we're not actually in school."

"We are sort of."

"I don't see that we are. I'd like to make a slide. Let's simply dash without saying anything."

"She'll shout after us."

"We can pretend not to hear. I'm going to. One—two—three—go!"

As she said it, she suddenly raced off ahead of the others, alone. Miss Rutter saw her, and called after her. Dorothy took no notice, but went on running down the lane towards the pond as fast as she could go. Miss Rutter called again. She was really annoyed now. It was one thing to have them play about, but quite another thing to have one of them flatly ignore her like this. She made a mental note that she would have to give Dorothy a punishment for this. She called again, but Dorothy was disappearing now round a bend in the lane. As she vanished from sight, Miss Rutter suddenly remembered exactly why she was walking along with the girls, why she had called for them all, why they were not allowed to be alone in the lanes for a moment. She started to quicken her steps forward. She overtook the crocodile and started to go on ahead of them. And then, from the distance, from beyond the bend, she heard a feeble, wailing little scream. The blood was pounding in her chest as she ran down the lane towards the bend.

TWO

James Wilson came to a little open patch in the scrub and gorse that grew all round. He paused for breath, and turned to look back across the strip that he had just been searching. Away to his left, about thirty yards away, another man was blundering through the scrub, prodding some of the bushes with a stick. Away to his right, another man did the same, using the butt of a twelve-bore gun to prod with. Beyond them, on either side, were other men, bending, peering, prodding, searching.

James Wilson gave his head a little shake of irritation. What they need on this job, he was thinking, is not me but a couple of genuine four-legged bloodhounds. That's what they need. A fat lot of good I am, now that it has turned out this way.

He smiled for a moment as he thought of what he had been doing the night before. Those questions. How these locals hated questions! Every time you questioned anyone, they thought you were trying to pin it on them. And yet they were so different from the fancy boys. The fancy boys always thought you were trying to pin something on them, because each of them knew that there was plenty that could be pinned on to them at any time. It wasn't like that with these people. They resented the hint of suspicion. They were all so honest that it stuck out a mile, but every time you asked a simple routine question they imagined they were being challenged. Well, you could have saved yourself the trouble, James Wilson told himself now. You didn't need clues after all. Not even alibis. You could have saved yourself the trouble if only you had known the fellow was going to be so obliging as to have another go and be spotted in the process. But you couldn't know that. Killers are not usually quite so helpful.

But it was lucky he did not finish the second one off. It was lucky for that Bond girl herself, but it was lucky for you too. You wouldn't have looked so big, mister clever-stick Wilson, if he had finished off another one right under your nose. But as it is, this fellow is going to be quite a useful, obliging sort of cuss. He's saved you the brain work. All you have to do now is to make an arrest and collect your witnesses. You're practically certain for top marks, ten out of ten. Very useful. Two or three of these will get you promotion the easy way.

He ran his eyes round in a circle, across the tops of the gorse bushes. You haven't got him yet, he reminded himself. Don't count the chickens yet. This stuff is thick in places, and a man might crawl into cover and take a bit of finding. These chaps are so blazing mad with fury that they're being more quick than thorough. And you didn't see him come this way yourself. You've only got the word of those two who say they saw him dive in here.

He walked across to the man on his right.

"This stuff is pretty close cover in places," James Wilson said. "I think there's a risk of us trying to comb it too quickly."

The man swung round on him, swinging his gun round too.

"You leave it to us!" he said fiercely.

James Wilson tilted his chin up a bit. He wasn't in the mood for being pushed around.

"I'm in charge of this," he said coldly.

For a moment he thought the man was going to club him with his gun. The man's voice came rasping and husky.

"I'm going to kill him for it," he said. "Nobody's going to stop me. I'm going to kill him. Merciful heaven—it was only by the grace of God that he didn't kill my little girl this morning."

James Wilson suddenly saw the things in his eyes, and the greyness of him, and the sagging of his cheeks. He had got the men mixed up, and he had not realised this was Bond. He shut his mouth and turned his head and looked the other way.

The crouching figure peered out from behind the trunk of a tree. He was in a small clump of trees that grew on the top of a slight rise in the ground. From where he was, he could look down across the gorse-covered stretch of common, and he could see the men, stretched out each side, kicking and prodding their way through the gorse, searching their way steadily towards the clump of trees where he was hiding. He did not like the look of those men.

He shivered slightly. It was very cold, staying still like this. But the cold was good. It made the ground all hard, so that nobody could follow your footprints. You could step right in the mud and even then you did not leave any mark, because the mud was not mud anymore, it was all so cold.

And the cold was good for other reasons too. It made your breath show when you breathed, and that was nice. You could make fairies when you breathed. Little cloudy fairies. One, two, three—very quickly—and there were three little cloudy fairies, chasing each other. They never quite caught each other, though. Just as you thought that the second one was going to catch the first one, the first one disappeared. And then just as you thought the third one was going to catch the second one, the second one disappeared. No matter how quickly you did it, they never quite caught up with each other.

That little girl this morning was like a fairy. But not like a breath-fairy. She didn't disappear before you could catch her. You thought she was going to, but she didn't. When you put out your hands to catch her, you could feel her in your hands, and so you knew she had not disappeared. But then that shouting interrupted you. You did not want people shouting at you. You wanted to make quite sure that she was not going to disappear, but they shouted at you and then you had to run away. That wasn't nice. But it was nice in another way, somehow. Because it meant you ran away before she stopped moving. It would not have been nice if she had stopped moving. The other one stopped moving, and that wasn't nice at all. That was horrible. She stopped moving, and that meant that she was dead. That was because you held her too long. When you hold them too long, they stop moving, and then it isn't nice. But this one did not stop moving. She was still moving when the people shouted at you and you had to run away. They could not catch you, because you ran so fast. You can run faster than anyone in the world. Nobody can run as fast as you. Nobody can catch you when you run. Even the breath-fairies get left miles behind. You can run so fast that it doesn't seem cold anymore.

Those men are looking for me now. They think I am hiding in those bushes down there. I'm not. I am hiding in these trees.

She will be so terribly cross with me when I get back. I had no business to come here at all. She made me promise that I would never go away. Not anywhere. I was supposed to stay right by there, right where she was. She made me promise, and when she asks me to do anything, I don't mind. I didn't mind promising her to stay there and not go away anywhere. She is so good, so beautiful, that I don't mind what I promise her. I could never say no to her. I would never want to say no to her. That is why I promised her that I wouldn't ever go away from there. And now she will be so terribly cross when I get back. She is so kind and so beautiful that I don't like making her cross or unhappy. But she will be cross and unhappy. Even if I had only come away from there, that would make her cross, because I promised not to. But when she hears about that little girl, about the way she stopped moving, about her being dead, then she will be terribly cross. I shall not like that. I hate it when she is cross with me, because she is so beautiful. As soon as I get back to her, I will promise her again. I will promise never, never, never to go away from there, away from her. I will really promise this time.

He suddenly switched his attention back to the men who were searching their way steadily towards him across the gorse-covered common. They were coming nearer, nearer. He could see them very clearly now. He could see that some of them had guns. He pressed himself against the trunk of the tree, and smiled. They thought he was hiding down there, somewhere in the bushes. But he wasn't. He was hiding up here in the trees. They would never guess that. They were silly. They did not run fast enough. They could not run half as fast as he could. Nobody could do that. It was nice when you were running. It stopped being cold then. The air was still cold enough for the breath-fairies to come out of your mouth, but your body was warm when you were running. It was cold now, because he wasn't running. You could not run now, because you were hiding up here in the trees, and you had to stand still for that. If you suddenly started running now, those men would see you. They thought you were hiding down there in the bushes, and they would never find you if you didn't suddenly run, because you were not down there in the bushes at all, you were up here in the trees. You could see them, but they couldn't see you. That made you cleverer than them. And you could run faster than they could, too. So you were cleverer than them in both ways. But she would be terribly cross all the same. She would not care about you being cleverer than them. That would not make any difference with her. She would be cross just the same. I did not want to make her cross. She is so beautiful. I'll really promise her this time. I really will.

They are coming through the bushes now. They are looking in all the bushes, and they are gradually coming nearer. Why don't they stop looking? I am in the trees, not in the bushes. Why don't they stop looking in the bushes? Why don't they stop looking and go away, right away? I don't want them to look for me. I don't want them to find me.

She will be cross if they find me. She will be crosser than ever if they find me. Terribly cross. I don't want them to find me. They mustn't find me.

What will they do if they find me? What will they do to me? They will hurt me. They will all be cross with me, and they will punish me and hurt me. Why does everybody have to be cross with me? They mustn't find me. I don't want anybody to hurt me.

They are coming nearer. Every time I look they are a little bit nearer. They are much nearer now. Why can't they stop looking? I am not down there in the bushes. They will not find me down there in the bushes. Why can't they go away, instead of coming nearer. They are nearer, much nearer. They are coming nearer all the time. Don't come any nearer! Go away! I don't want you to come any nearer!

If they keep on coming nearer, they will find me. They are gradually coming nearer to me. That one with the gun is coming slowly towards me, straight towards me. If they come much nearer they will find me. Please don't let them find me.

Please! Please don't let them find me. She will be cross. I don't want anyone to find me. I don't want anyone to hurt me. Please don't come any nearer. Please! Nobody find me. Nobody catch me. Please! No! No!

He broke suddenly from the cluster of trees, and rushed down the slope in frantic flight. He steered away from where the men were, away down the other side of the slope to where it was open grassland. The shouts had started the moment he moved, and as he left the cover of the trees two bangs in quick succession came from somewhere to the right. The sounds were sharpened by the frosty air, and seemed to come from closer than they really were. They pinged in his ears and sent him forward faster still. He felt nothing, saw nothing, and prayed that he was out of shotgun range.

He ran blindly forward, making for nowhere, making only away from what was behind him. He wrenched all the speed he could find in those long, loose legs. The ground was frozen hard, and he seemed to skim across it. His mouth was wide open, and as he sucked in fiercely, the icy cold air pricked his lungs like a knife.

He turned his head quickly to look behind him as he ran. He saw the pack of wolves, shouting, barking, coming in full flight after him.

He heard again the quick bang-bang of another two barrels. He ran faster still. A hedge stretched across in front of him, and he went straight at it. Without even checking his speed he flung himself upwards and forwards, crashing his feet through the top of the intertwined twigs. It was not such a very high hedge, and he could have cleared it if only he had taken a moment to time it and judge it properly. But he tried to take it in full stride, and his feet crashed through the top of it and hooked in something. His body went forward in a downward arc with all the force of the speed at which he had been travelling. His head crashed down on to the frozen earth. It felt like butting a lump of jagged cast iron. For a moment he was standing on his head, and then his feet came unhooked and his legs came crumpling down on top of the rest of him.

For a moment he lay there, conscious only of a billowing thunder-noise in his head, loud-soft, loud-soft, loud-soft. And then he heard the shouts again. He struggled to his feet, dizzy and hardly knowing anything at all. He did not know which way he had been running, but he set off again blindly, only knowing that he had to get away. He ran with every breath of desperate energy he could find. His head was throbbing, and in spite of the cold one side of his face was burning hot.

He ran with the frenzied effort that kills a runner. His heart was pounding. The blood was pressing up into his eyes. A frightening tightness was wrapping itself around his chest. He felt that if he stopped for a moment he would never go on again. But he did not stop. The only thing he knew was that he had to get away, and he went on running, faster, faster. His legs were moving mechanically now. There wasn't any conscious physical effort anymore. There was only the drumming, deafening will, the will to get away.

The sounds behind him grew gradually more vague and distant. He gradually threw off the creepy feeling that hands were about to grab him from behind. He jerked another look over his shoulder, and felt a surge of satisfaction. He could run faster than anyone else in the world.

He went through a gate and came on to a lane. He was past any thought of taking cover or hiding. He was like a river that has burst the dam. He was on the run, and nothing could make him stop.

He turned along the lane, running straight along the middle crest of it, not even bothering to make use of the screening he could have had by running close to one of the hedges. He had no thought of hiding anymore. Hiding was over. Hiding was standing still and getting cold because you were not running. Now he was running and he was warm again, and he did not want to think about hiding, not even by running close to one of the hedges. The surface of the lane was smoother than the frozen nobbly fields, and now those lanky legs took on a smoother rhythm. His arms moved backwards and forwards in time with his legs. They moved like the pistons of an engine. He was going forward swiftly, smoothly, just like a train. That was what he was now. He was a train. Pheeeeep! Pheeeeeep! He was a train now. Nobody get on the line, because he was a train and he only stopped for signals. There would not be any signals against him, either, because he was an express. Out of his mouth, into the frosty air, came the quickly regular puffs of steam. The trees at the side of the road were the telegraph poles, flashing by regularly. The lane that stretched ahead of him was the gleaming double metal track of the main line. He was a train all right. Those men behind would never catch him now. How could they? He was a train, an express train, and they were only running.

The lane started to curve and wind suddenly. He was running gradually slower now, his breath pumping deeper and deeper with the long effort. He saw the sharp twists and turns in the lane, and knew that a main line did not twist about like that. He could not be an express train if he had to keep turning round sharp bends. He would stop being an express train, and be a motor car instead. That was better. Now he was a motor car. They still would not catch him, because they were on foot and he was a motor car. It was better being a motor car. He did not have to keep to the lines in the centre of the lane anymore. Now that he was a motor car, he could wrench the wheel suddenly over and cut the corners closely.

As he rounded another corner, he saw ahead of him, about half a mile along the lane, a small village made up of a few straggling cottages. He slowed suddenly, hesitating, wondering whether to dive through the hedge and take to the fields again. But as he hesitated, he saw something ahead of him that drew him forward irresistibly. It was a car, pulling up outside one of the cottages in the village. As he kept running forward along the lane, he saw a man get out of the car, open the front gate to the garden of the cottage, walk to the cottage and go in through the door. The loping figure ran on down the lane. He was tiring badly now, gasping for breath, but he forced himself forward in a sudden swift spurt. He could drive a car. That was just what he wanted, a real car instead of just pretending to be one. If he could take that car, he could get home quickly, without any chance of being followed, without any risk of being caught.

He ran on down the lane. The view of the village and the standing car was suddenly less distinct as the air was filled with gusting flakes of snow. There was nobody in sight as he approached the car. He ran straight up to it, not waiting to look around him. He opened the door and slipped into the driving seat. It was an ancient Morris, one of the makes he knew how to drive. He pressed the starter button and the engine started straight away. He pulled back the gear lever and let in the clutch with a jerk. As he heard a furious shout from the cottage, the car moved off. He accelerated quickly and changed the gears up, and as the car went swiftly forward he laughed to himself out loud. Nobody could ever catch him now. Nobody could even follow him or guess which way he had gone. He laughed again. He was cleverer than they were.

He drove as fast as the car would go, straight along the road out of the village. As he passed clear of the last of the straggling cottages, he turned his head to take a quick look out of the little back window of the car. He could see the owner of the car, standing in the middle of the road, helplessly shaking his fist after him. He crouched forward in the driving seat, urging the car forward, laughing with delight at his own cleverness. Those first gusting flakes of snow were getting bigger now, and he put one hand up to the top of the windscreen and fiddled with the windscreen wiper. It suddenly started to flip quickly to and fro, sweeping a clear little arc in the snow that was collecting on the glass. He leaned his head forward, near to the windscreen, to give himself a better view as he drove along. They would never catch him now, he was thinking. Nobody would find him, nobody would catch him, nobody would be able to hurt him now.

The snow came swirling round the car, and started to settle lightly on the surface of the road. The tread of the tires bit through the thin white film, and left two long, unbroken trails on the road behind him.

THREE

James Wilson had never completely lost track of him. When that flying figure had crashed through the top of the hedge and hurtled to the ground, lying there seemingly stunned for several seconds, James Wilson had really thought that the chase was over. He had forced himself into an extra spurt, and had just been approaching the hedge when the fugitive had suddenly picked himself up and gone tearing ahead again. That extra spurt had made James Wilson ease up a little after that. He was good on his feet, but he knew that he was no real match for that loping, bounding, speeding thing ahead of him. But he had never completely lost track. He was way out in front of the rest of the searchers. They were straggled out unevenly, at various distances behind. Some of the fools had been popping off their guns, without the slightest chance of hitting what they were presumably aiming at. It wasn't any too cosy being the fastest runner of this bunch, James Wilson thought. It meant you stood quite a good chance of getting your backside filled with buckshot.

From the hedge, that scrambling figure had drawn steadily ahead again, inch by inch, yard by yard. James Wilson was putting everything he had into it, but he could not stop the gap between them from lengthening. Two hedges further on he had lost sight of the quarry, then glimpsed it again, then lost it again. But he had never completely lost track. The figure ahead seemed to be running blindly, thinking only of his speed and not much of his direction. James Wilson had seen him reach the road and turn to the right along it. The course of the road was shown by the trees that seemed to run along beside it, and James Wilson had immediately swung slantingly away to the right, not following directly, but making a long third side to a triangle, aiming for the furthest point at which he could still see the trees that flanked the road. He knew he would save himself something like a quarter of a mile by doing that, unless the other man broke away from the road somewhere on the far side of it. He ran steadily, with long, easy strides. He did not know how long this was going on, and he did not want to use up everything too soon.

He reached the road through the yard at the side of a farmhouse.

The snow was beginning to swirl in his face as he stumbled over the iron-hard mud and dung. He was just at the beginning of the village. He had caught up more than he knew by taking that slanting course. He turned to the right and saw a man in the middle of the road, shouting and shaking his fist at apparently nothing. And then, through the vague white mist of the falling snow, James Wilson could just see the back of a car disappearing into the distance.

He panted up to the man in the middle of the road.

"Has a man just come through here, running fast?" He asked the question in a series of jerking gasps.

The man in the road turned to look at him for a moment, and then looked ahead down the road again.

"Running be damned," he said disgustedly. "He's pinched my car!"

James Wilson glanced quickly at the straggling cottages along each side of the road. Then he turned to the man again.

"Who else in this village has got a car?" he asked quickly.

The man turned round and faced him squarely. "Look here," he began. "If this chap who's pinched my car is a friend of yours, you'd better—"

James Wilson cut in on him.

"I'm a police officer in plain clothes," he said curtly. "I want to know where I can find a car in this village. I want it quickly. I've got to catch that man." He jerked his head in the direction that the other car had gone.

The man in the road had changed his manner the moment he had heard the words police officer. Now he quickly glanced around him, full of important excitement. He pointed back to the farm at the beginning of the village.

"Bert Tulley's'll be there," he said. "It'll be in his shed there."

"Show me," James Wilson told him, speaking back over his shoulder as he started running back towards the farm. The other man ran back following him. When they reached the farm, the man ran up to the door of the farmhouse and hammered on it with his fist. A woman opened the door.

"Afternoon, Mr. Rich," she said, and then looked beyond him, questioningly, seeing a stranger there.

"We want to borrow Bert's car," the man said to her. "Tell him we had to borrow it, will you?"

He moved away from the door towards a shed beside the house, not waiting for the woman to give permission. She frowned quickly, resenting the assumption, and called after him.

"I don't know as Bert will want you to take it just now," she said. "He may be wanting it himself as soon as he gets back in."

James Wilson turned to her, and politely but quickly told her who he was. She looked awed and rather frightened. The man was pulling open the doors of the shed, and James Wilson went across and pushed in past him, and got into the car and turned the switch and pressed the starter. He saw the petrol indicator flip well up, and the engine started quickly. He backed the car out of the shed and across the yard towards the gate. As he swung it round backwards into the road, someone panted up heavily and pulled open the door on the other side of the car.

"Where'd he go?"

James Wilson jerked his head round quickly and saw Bond there.

"Look out," he said. "Stand away. I'm going. I'm after him."

He let in the clutch to drive forward. Bond flung himself through the door on to the seat beside him. Bond was very nearly blown. His breath was coming in uneven gasps, and his face was very red. As the car moved forward, he pulled his feet in through the door, and pulled the door shut. James Wilson felt something hard hit against his shoulder. He looked and saw that it was the barrel of Bond's gun. He put the car into top gear, and drove it forward through the swirling snow. The tracks of the other car were already softened over by the fresh flakes, but they were still clearly visible. He pushed the car forward as fast as he could make it go.

Bond was still puffing and blowing by his side. He must have very nearly run himself out.

"Point that gun somewhere else," James Wilson said.

Bond moved the gun, shoving the butt down on the floor of the car between his legs, with the barrels pointing straight up in front of him.

"How do you know which way he's gone?" Bond asked.

"He pinched a car. I didn't miss him by much. These are his tracks on the road."

"Drive faster."

"It won't go any faster. The engine's cold." He did not like the way Bond had said it. It sounded as if he was giving him orders.

"How far are we behind him?" Bond asked.

"I shouldn't think more than ten minutes. It might be less. But I don't know what sort of a car he has got. This one is not much good."

"We must catch him. It will be dark soon. We must catch him before it gets dark. Why don't you go faster?"

"I tell you it won't go any faster. Do you think I'm driving along here for fun, anyway?"

James Wilson was beginning to hold the wheel gingerly. The ground had been frozen hard for days, and the snow was settling firmly on it. The corners were getting slippery. He was thinking that soon they would have to be going slower, not faster.

"I followed you," Bond was saying. "I didn't see him again after the first few minutes, but I managed to keep you in sight. How near did you get to him?"

"I nearly caught him when he tripped over one of the first hedges. I thought I was going to get him then. But he's fast on his feet all right."

"Did you see who it was? Did you see his face?"

"No. I only saw the back of him. I didn't even see much of his head. He leans forward in a peculiar way while he's running."

Bond said: "It's a crying pity you hadn't got a gun. You could have shot him. You must have been near enough for that."

James Wilson laughed.

"I'm not trying to shoot him," he said. "I'm trying to catch him."

"It's the same thing," said Bond.

"How do you make that out?"

It was Bond who laughed this time. But there was not any humour in the laugh. It was not so much a laugh as a quick succession of jerky, threatening sounds.

"It comes to the same thing," said Bond.

"Not with me," James Wilson answered. He was straining forward to watch the road and his whole concentration was taken up by the driving. But he could feel the tenseness of the man beside him, the fierce determination, the threat in the voice. James Wilson shrugged his shoulders. It was always the same, it was always a nuisance if things happened to go like this. You always had to shake the people off before you could do any thinking, before you could do anything clear and straight. To him it was just a job, and up to now a ridiculously easy one. But to the man beside him it was not like that, it was something very different. You had to shake off the people like that, or wait till they had cooled down if you had time. You couldn't join in. You had to be careful and firm about not throwing your sympathies around. If you allowed your mind to get mixed up with the tempers and griefs and excitements that were always there, it simply meant you were softening on the job. It meant in the end that you probably mucked the job too. He turned his head to glance at Bond. That one had not cooled down yet. He hadn't even started.

The snow was now falling steadily and heavily, in big flakes that lay thickly over the road and the hedges and the fields. It was plastered in a thick mat over the windscreen, broken by the two smeary arcs of the twin wipers. Their breath was condensing on the inside of the glass, and every few minutes they had to wipe it with their hands to enable them to see anything at all. James Wilson was pressing the car along as fast as he could and as fast as he dared. The snow on the road was thickening rapidly and in places it was not very easy to see where the road ended and the ditches began. He could still see the tracks of the car ahead of them. The tracks were dulled over by the fresh snow on top of them, but the shape of the indentation was still there. It was almost impossible to tell from the appearance of the tracks whether they were gaining on the other car or losing. The snow was drifting, and every few yards the tracks on the road were different. Sometimes they looked as if they had been made a few moments before, and at other times the snow had drifted heavily over them so that they were almost invisible. As the snow became thicker the speed of the car became gradually less. It was difficult to see through that swirling whiteness, but they seemed to be going steadily uphill. It was mostly second-gear work now, and the wheels kept trying to spin.

Bond was peering forward with his face almost touching the glass of the windscreen.

"We're not catching him," he muttered. "He'll be going faster than this. We're almost crawling along now. Why don't you go faster? Go faster!"

They had been travelling for nearly an hour. The light was fading, but with the whiteness all over the ground it did not seem dark. It was the whirling white of the snowflakes that made it difficult to see.

"Have you any idea where we're getting to?" James Wilson asked.

"We're beginning to get up into the hills," Bond said. "I don't know this part much myself. There's no town this way for a good long stretch. It gets pretty desolate up towards the top here."

"Where do you think he can be heading for?" Bond made a noise like spitting.

"Just running," he said. "That's all he's doing. Get a move on, can't you? We'll never catch him at this rate."

The snow was getting steadily deeper, and it was falling so thickly through the air now that it seemed to make an almost solid wall in front of them. The windscreen wipers kept jamming against the piled-up snow on the outside of the glass, and they had to keep reaching their arms out through the windows to knock the snow away.

James Wilson was beginning to shiver with the cold. The pursuit had gone on too long, and was getting too much of a crawl, for the mental excitement to keep the cold away. The chase across the fields and through the hedges had soaked his underwear with sweat, and now it was lying chillingly against his skin. As he sat in the seat of the car he could feel the heartening pressure against his hip of the flat half bottle of whisky in his pocket. It had been so cold the night before that he had bought it at the local pub against emergency. It was just what he needed at the moment, but he could not stop for it now. And by the look of things, there would be plenty more use for it later on. It looked as if he was going to be cold for a long time yet.

The road was getting steeper. They were climbing all the time. The snow was banking high in places, first on one side of the road, then on the other. The tracks were harder to follow now, but they passed no turns off the road so they knew the other car must still be ahead. With that blinding swirl in front of them, it was hard to see enough to steer clear of the drifts on the sides of the road.

"This is some snowstorm," James Wilson said.

"Faster. Go faster!" The man beside him was still straining himself forward, as if trying to project himself along faster than the speed of the car.

James Wilson suddenly felt the steering wheel pull heavily sideways. He wrenched at it to keep it straight, but the pull was too strong for him. He lifted his foot quickly off the accelerator, but he was not quite quick enough. As the piled snow trapped one of the front wheels and pulled it to the side, there was a whirr from the engine as the back wheels went into a spin. The back of the car came round in a sudden vicious swing, bringing it broadside across the road. As the accelerator came up, the force of the skid wrenched the whole car backwards. For a moment it was completely out of control. Then they were both thrown heavily sideways as the back of the car fetched up solidly against something behind.

Muttering to himself, James Wilson sat back in his seat, and very deliberately pulled the gear into neutral, pressed the starter button, felt the gear lever gently into bottom, took a firm hold of the wheel, and let the clutch in as steadily as he could. As the clutch pedal came right home the purr of the engine was joined by the whine of the gear-box, but the car did not move. It just gave a couple of shudders and settled itself down comfortably.

Bond was out of the car first. Gripping his gun, he was out of the car and several yards further along the road before James Wilson realised what he was doing. From the look of him, crouching forward and holding his gun at the ready, it was as if he had just had a glimpse through the snow of the man he was after. He looked like a man who was expecting to pull the trigger at any moment. James Wilson fell out of the door of the car and went racing after him. Bond was about twenty-five yards away up the road, and with the snow swirling so thickly that was as far as you could see. Lifting his feet high to climb through the snow, James Wilson struggled forward to catch that threatening figure ahead of him. It took him a good five minutes to make up the twenty-five yards' difference. He was shouting after him all the time, but Bond took no notice. When at last he caught him up, he had to grab Bond's arm to make him take any notice. He could tell now, by the way Bond's eyes were vaguely searching from side to side, that he had not sighted anyone yet.

He tugged at Bond's arm roughly.

"What's the idea?" he demanded. "Do you think I can pull that car out on my own?"

Bond pulled his arm away, and peered again into the swirling snow ahead of him. He swung the gun in an arc that followed where his eyes were going.

"He might be anywhere here," he muttered. "He might be skulking anywhere here."

James Wilson caught hold of his arm again and shook it.

"Don't be a fool!" he said sharply. "We haven't caught up with his car yet. Do you think you are going to catch it up on foot? Come back and help me see if we can shift the car out of the snow. Buck up. You're only wasting time doing this."

Bond tried to pull his arm away from James Wilson's grasp.

"The car's bogged up," he said. "We haven't got time to mess about with that. We must keep after him. Keep after him. We must not give him a chance."

"You must be mad!" James Wilson told him fiercely. "He may be five miles away from here. The snow is so patchy it's impossible to say how far he may manage to get with the car. Our only chance is to get that car shifted out of the snow."

Bond suddenly saw the sense of this, and turned round quickly and went back towards their car as fast as he could. Together they peered round the back of it and under the wheels. The back of the body had rammed itself up against a solid wall of drifted snow, and that had saved it from going off the roadway altogether. But the bumpers and fenders had dug down into the drift, so that now they were trapped by a barrier of snow in front of them. The two back wheels had very nearly buried themselves.

Bond started trying to push the car out, with a kind of childish, petulant impatience.

"Clear from underneath the bumpers first," James Wilson said. "Then we'll get those chunks from under the fenders. It's no good trying to get her going while there's all that holding her back."

They shovelled with their hands and pushed with the soles of their shoes. It was difficult work without a spade. Bond was muttering all the time about the time they were losing. He worked quickly, furiously. Now he had started on the job he tackled it like a giant. He had finished his side before James Wilson had cleared his.

"Now get it away from just in front of the back wheels," James Wilson said. "But mind you don't harden it down there too much. I suppose there aren't any chains in this car?"

He stopped working suddenly as he thought of the possibility of there being some chains. He was cursing himself for not looking before, as he pulled open the boot at the back of the car and scuffled around in the untidy muddle of tools and jack and petrol can. There were no chains there. He climbed into the back of the car and lifted the seat away to look behind it. There were no chains.

He got out again and inspected the lie of the car very carefully. He knew that if they made a false try, and got the wheels spinning fast again, they would be dug in again as badly as ever in a matter of seconds. He fetched out the wide leather seat from the back of it. He propped this against the wall of snow behind the back wheels. If Bond tried to push from behind, his feet would simply keep sinking into the snow. But the wide flat surface of the leather seat would press firmly against the snow bank and give him something to push against.

He told Bond: "Get that seat resting evenly against the snow. Then put your feet against it and get ready to push. Don't push till I say so. I want your whole energy at the moment I let the clutch in. If she'll take the first few inches then she'll get away all right. But if we get her moving then it's best to keep her moving. If she goes, then I'll keep crawling along the road in the hope that you can catch up and jump in."

Bond got his feet against the leather seat and braced himself ready to push. James Wilson was just going to get into the car when he paused and held out his hand.

"Better give me that gun," he said. "You can push better and catch up better if you're not bothering with that."

Bond held the gun tightly.

"I'm keeping this," he said. "I'm not letting go of this. I'll need it soon."

"You don't need it to push with. It'll only get in your way. I'll put it in the car."

Bond hesitated, and then held it out to him. Even when James Wilson had taken hold of it, Bond did not leave go for a second or two. He seemed resentful and suspicious at letting it go out of his hands. James Wilson laid it on the floor in the back of the car, and slipped into the driving seat.

"Don't push till I shout," he said.

He switched on the engine and started it up, and then pushed out the clutch and put the gear in. Keeping the engine running fairly slowly, he eased the clutch pedal back gently until he could feel it trying to bite.

"Now!" he shouted through the window, and let the clutch come all the way. He felt the wheels spin for a moment, and then the car shuddered and suddenly jerked forward. He pulled the steering wheel gently round, and the car slithered on to the top of the road, wandered a bit and then gradually straightened and then went crawling forward with the wheels biting properly. He kept the car moving as slowly as he dared. He knew that if he stopped it he might have trouble in getting it moving again. Before he had gone many yards he felt the jolt of Bond landing on the running board. Bond managed to open the door, and tumbled in on to the seat beside him.

"Nice work," said James Wilson.

Bond was already leaning backwards over the seat and groping on the floor of the car for his gun. He found it and lifted it over, and held it between his knees again.

"We'll never catch him now," he said. "Go as fast as you can."

For a moment James Wilson had almost forgotten about the man ahead whom they were chasing. This battle with the swirling and drifting snow was threatening to become a whole-time occupation in itself. The immediate things, such as getting the car going again, steering a course through the drifts on either side of the road, and trying to peer through the blinding whiteness in front of them, were enough to take all the attention. It seemed an almost unreal job, trying to catch up with the other car. The real thing that needed all his concentration was to keep their own car going. They were both of them white from head to foot from standing in the snowstorm while they dug the car out. The thought crossed James Wilson's mind that if they wanted to turn round and go back they would probably not be able to get through.

"We're all of us going to get nicely snowed up soon," he said to Bond.

"I'll catch him first," Bond answered. "I'll catch him first if I have to walk through it all night."

"That car he pinched must be fitted with snow shoes."

"I can't see his tracks at all now," said Bond. "He must be a long way in front of us for his tracks to get covered right over."

"I don't know. At the rate it's coming down and drifting, anything could get blotted out in a few minutes. We could probably see something if we got out of the car, but I don't like to stop it. We might not get it started again."

Bond tried sticking his head out through the window and looking down at the ground, but the snow came blinding into his face and it was worse that way.

"He may have dodged us," he said. "He may not have come this way at all."

"He must have come this way. Since we last saw his tracks, there's not been any turning off this road. I'm certain of that. His car must still be in front of us. And if his car is in front of us, so is he."

As Bond heard the definite sureness of James Wilson's voice, he gripped his gun firmly and raised it up a bit. He would have held it pointing ahead along the road if the glass windscreen had not been in the way.

They had been in the car for some hours now. It would have been quite dark but for the whiteness of the snow. James Wilson did not know how far they had come. He had not noted the mileage on the speedometer when they started. But he noticed now that the petrol needle indicated at least five gallons less than it had at the start. The low gear driving had been eating it up. There were only two or three gallons left.

"There must have been plenty of petrol in that car he pinched," he said. "We'll be getting low soon."

But he was not really thinking that it was the petrol that was going to stop them. The snow was regularly piling up against the wheels now. It was steadily getting thicker everywhere. His arms were aching with the effort to hold the wheels straight. He knew it could not be long before they got bogged up for good.

From the feel of the car it seemed as if they had stopped climbing and were on a level stretch of road. The swirling whiteness only allowed him to see enough to keep on the road and out of the drifts. He could not see the shape of the countryside. There was only the feel of the car to tell him. The pull of the engine was just the same because of the piling snow pushing backwards against the wheels, but now the slithering was tending to be forwards instead of from side to side. He thought they were on a level stretch, but the pull of the snow and the short visibility made him keep in low gear. It seemed to be slithering more than ever now. It was slithering forwards in sudden convulsive jerks. He eased his foot right off the accelerator, and gripped the wheel instinctively tighter as he felt the car going forward of its own accord. He touched the footbrake, very gingerly. It seemed to make no difference. The car was going faster, faster, and he suddenly realised from the angle of the seat that they were going steeply downhill. The back wheels slewed round so that they were diagonally across the road. The whole thing was sidling forwards like a crab, faster every moment. He pulled at the steering wheel, trying to get the car straight again. The wheel was useless in his hands. He turned it still further, trying to coax it out of the skid. The car suddenly came round viciously, right round, so that it was moving broadside on the other tack. He felt Bond thrown against him by the quick lunge of the car.

"Look out where you're going!" he heard Bond say.

James Wilson suddenly knew that the thing had got too much for him and he was not going to be able to hold it or pull it out or stop it. All he could do was to tug at the wheel and try to ram into one of the drifts at the side to stop the car. It seemed to be going faster and the angle was getting steeper, and the tugging at the wheel didn't do anything at all. He tried the other way, and then the other way, and then he did not know which way he had the wheels turned, and the car was going backwards now, straight backwards, tilting him back in his seat, faster, sickeningly faster, downwards, dropping away from him, with no direction and nothing to see except the blinding swirling whiteness blotting out the windows. And then he felt the back of the seat punch him just below the shoulder blades, and then he jerked forward and took the steering wheel hard in the pit of his stomach.

All he knew about for the next few moments was the sound of breaking glass and the feeling that he wanted to be sick. He knew that the car was not moving anymore, and he turned his head to look at Bond, and Bond was leaning forward and seemed to be very still, and then the feeling of wanting to be sick was bigger than ever, it was the most important of everything, it was really all he knew about now, and he fumbled with the catch on the door beside him, and pushed the door open and leaned out over the snow and let it all go.

It was over and out of him quickly, and it faded away just as suddenly as it had come, and he turned the other way to look at Bond again. Bond was not so still now. He was feeling his chin, rubbing it in a dazed kind of way. James Wilson could see that the windscreen in front of Bond was shattered to bits. He leaned across to him.

"Where'd it get you?" he asked. The sickness was floating back at him as he spoke.

Bond shook himself. His voice sounded rather bewildered.

"I think I knocked myself out on my gun," he said.

James Wilson looked at the broken glass.

"Have you cut yourself?" he asked. It was difficult to see.

"I don't think so," Bond told him. "I put the barrel through the windscreen, that's all."

Bond was rapidly getting everything back. His voice was firmer all the time.

"I should think that's the end of our motoring for tonight," James Wilson said.

The sound of his words seemed to bring Bond back to his senses and strength with a jolt. He straightened himself and forced away the last traces of dizziness that the bang on his jaw had given him. He turned to unfasten the door on his side of the car.

"Come on. Quick. We're wasting time. Let's get after him." He did not even think to ask if James Wilson was all right.

He pulled back the catch of the door, and pushed against it with his shoulder. He swore, and pushed against it with all his weight, but it would not go open. Then he looked through the window and saw that the snow was piled up like a high wall against it. He swung round in his seat.

"Try your side," he said.

The door on James Wilson's side was already open from his leaning out to be sick. He was still feeling wobbly down inside him, and just for the moment he was not in a hurry to move. But when Bond tried to squeeze across between him and the steering wheel, squashing against his stomach in the process, he rolled out of the car quickly, and stood in the thick snow, bending forward, holding his stomach, waiting for another relief.

Bond scrambled through the door, pulling his gun out after him.

"Where are we?" he asked. "Are we still on the road?"

James Wilson stood there, leaning forward, and quietly became sick again. It made him feel better.

He took off his gloves, and moved a few yards to make sure it would be clean snow, and scooped some up in his hand and washed his mouth and his chin with it, and took some into his mouth and tongued it around his teeth and spat it out again. It hurt his teeth and it made his face ache, but it made him feel cleaner and better. Then he pulled the flat half-bottle of whisky from his hip pocket and swallowed a little. It went roaring down into his stomach, and he was not quite sure if it was a good thing or a bad thing, but at least it made him feel a bit warmer inside.

He put the bottle back in his pocket, and took a good grip on himself and pushed the sickness right away. Then he turned to look at the car, to see what the chances were. It did not take more than a glance to see that there were no chances at all. Even if nothing was broken, the car was bedded and tilted in so that it would take a couple of horses or a tractor to shift it back into use.

The lights of the car had gone out. It seemed a lot darker without them, but it was still the swirling snow that was more of a barrier than the darkness. He pulled a torch from his pocket, but as soon as he switched it on it started to fade to a useless little glow. He had run the battery out with all his snooping around the night before. He put it back in his pocket and started to peer his way across the track along which the car had come. The whiteness showed the ground up easily, and a torch was not really necessary. The car had left a clear enough trail on its mad career down the slope. Just beyond the trail the ground appeared to drop away, and then there was a line of trees. He let his breath out deeply as he realised the car had stayed on the road by pure chance. It could just as easily have edged to the right a bit and somersaulted over.

But it was bad enough, James Wilson reminded himself quickly. They were stuck here good and proper. They were stuck here in a lonely part of the hills, miles from anywhere, in the middle of the heaviest snowstorm he had ever seen in England. And the snow was coming down in a way that looked as if it never meant to stop.

He suddenly realised that Bond had disappeared. He looked all round him quickly. The dancing whiteness seemed to close him in, and he could not see far. He called Bond's name. His voice was a lonely sound in that deadened silence. The snow seemed to soften the word and push it back at him. He shouted it louder, but still he got no answer.

He went back close to the car, and found the deep footprints that Bond had made, leading away in the direction of the road. He cupped his hands in that direction and shouted again, but nothing came back.

He looked at the footprints and muttered a few names for Bond. He turned, and knocked the snow from the running board of the car and squatted down and lighted a cigarette. But the snowflakes kept settling on the cigarette, making it hiss and splutter and draw badly, until he snatched it from his mouth and flung it away.

The only sensible thing to do was to get into the car and try to make themselves as warm as possible for the rest of the night. They were white with snow already, and if they didn't get under cover soon the snow would wriggle through their clothes and by the morning they would both have pneumonia. He would, anyway. Perhaps this fellow Bond was one of those hardened country people who didn't notice the weather. Bond hadn't had the steering wheel in the stomach, either. All right, if Bond wanted to go floundering off in the snow for the rest of the night, he could do it alone.

All the same, he isn't doing it just for a pleasure outing, remember. That was his kid this morning. Now wait a minute, James Wilson told himself sharply. Don't let yourself get going on this sentimental stuff. You'd better forget about him being the father. You'd better get that right out of your mind, and keep it out. Just because Bond happens to have been in the car with you, that's no reason for you to get hotted up about things. Everyone who gets attacked has a father or mother or a wife or a husband or a sister or a somebody. That's the first lesson you have to learn. You learned it long ago. All right. But it's a hard lesson too.

Anyway, this sort of stuff is not in your line. You're only supposed to be a detective, not a north-west Mountie or a polar explorer. They sent you on this job to see how you'd shape in a different sort of setting. Well, you don't shape. Not in this blizzard. The fellow can keep, until the morning, or until the snow melts. He'll probably perish to death in the storm, anyway. Then all you've got to do is go and arrest a dead body.

He could not have got much farther than this, though. Nobody could have got a car very much farther through this. It's thicker every minute. He can't be such a very long way ahead.

James Wilson looked down again at the footprints Bond had left. Already the freshly fallen snow had dimmed their first clear outline. Supposing Bond caught him, he thought. He won't, but just supposing he did. You wouldn't look so big then, would you? That wouldn't sound so good back at the office. Supposing Bond caught him and took him straight back in, missing you in the storm and taking him straight back in alone? That would look wonderful. That would look just fine.

He scowled down at the footprints and shook his head. Nobody was going to find anybody while this storm lasted.

This was the first time, he reflected, that he had chased a double murderer. Well, the second one wasn't killed, but that was only because of interruptions. They didn't grow double on every tree. And they certainly didn't often try to turn themselves into doubles under your nose, like this one. But you couldn't make guesses with these maniac people. One, two, three, four, it made no difference to them. They just got the habit.

He suddenly stood up, bolt upright, stiff and taut all over. He looked at the footprints and felt a tingling feeling up his spine. A spasm of fear made his heart pump harder. He set off along the blurring footprints. He ran, climbed, slithered, floundered along them as fast as he could go.

He knew it was the sickness from the wheel in his stomach that had made him lie down on the job for these few minutes. But that was no excuse. Already a kid had been nearly murdered almost under his nose. Somewhere, not far ahead, a maniac killer was lurking in the snow, and he had allowed this Bond, this blundering misery-blinded Bond to go after him alone. He hurled himself forward through the snow along the line of the footprints. The snow was half-way up his legs in places, and he seemed to be making no progress at all. He wrenched at his legs and scrambled and shovelled his way forward with desperate effort.

He suddenly stopped, and stood still, listening. It came again. A shout.

He tensed himself and struggled on again. It had not come from very far away. He held his hands ready for anything as he ploughed his way on through the blinding snow.

He nearly bumped into Bond. They were both so white with snow that they could hardly see each other. Bond was coming back towards him, shouting for him.

"I've found his car!" Bond gasped.

The relief at seeing Bond was pushed out of the way by what he said. He turned to plunge back through the snow, the way he had come from. James Wilson followed, keeping close behind him. They padded through the deep footprints that Bond had already made. Bond suddenly stopped, and pointed into the swirling thick whiteness of the snow. For a moment James Wilson could see nothing there. It was all just the same whiteness everywhere. And then he could make out a vague mounding shape standing out from the snowdrift. A small patch of black showed where Bond had knocked the snow away to make sure what it was. The shape of the thing was so thickly covered that it was hardly recognisable as a car. As they stepped up beside it they plunged in nearly up to their knees.

"This must be it," Bond said. His voice was not absolutely sure. As they stood and looked at that deeply bedded car, it seemed as if it must have been there for days. It seemed impossible that this could be the car that had only had a few miles start on them.

James Wilson was hurriedly trying to check it in his head. Through being behind all the time, they had had more snow to deal with all the way. That had been clear from the way the tracks of the car they had been following had been blurred and sometimes completely hidden. That meant the other car would have had it easier all the way, and would have been steadily gaining on them. The original few miles start would have been doubled, perhaps trebled. Then they had lost quite a lot of time getting themselves out of that first pile-up. The lead of the other car might have increased to an hour or even more. The weight of the snow that was coming down, and the way it was gusting and drifting fiercely, could cover almost anything in an hour.

The car was pointing off the road, with the front dipped down as if it had slithered into a ditch. James Wilson knocked the snow away from the window, and peered inside. There was nothing there to help him. He clambered his way round to the front of the car, and pushed his hand through the snow to feel the radiator. It was cold, but it could not be anything else with the snow all round and over it. But the snow seemed a good deal thinner on top of the bonnet, as it would be if the engine had been hot while the snow was first trying to settle on it.

"It's almost certain to be his," James Wilson said. "It's hardly likely that there would be another one stuck here."

"But where's he gone?" Bond demanded. "Where are his footprints? There are no footprints leading away from it at all."

James Wilson suddenly noticed that one of the doors, the one against the driving seat, was slightly open. The snow was piled almost as high inside the crack as outside. He pointed it out to Bond.

"That's why," he said. "There's been a sudden heavy drift here since the car stopped. Eight or ten inches have piled up here while that door has been standing open. That's why there aren't any footprints left. He probably skidded on the same steep slope that we skidded down, but the drift that stopped us was not there then, and he came right down to here and put his front wheels in the ditch."

"Well, where's he gone?" Bond asked again. He seemed to think James Wilson ought to know. They examined the surface of the snow carefully all round the buried car. There was not a sign of any trail in any direction. Whatever marks there might have been earlier had been completely blotted out.

"Where's he gone?" Bond asked again. His voice had a note of almost childish petulance, as if he felt that the information was being deliberately held back from him.

"He probably went straight on along the road," James Wilson guessed.

"He might not have done. He might have thought he could hide better by going away from the road."

"I shouldn't think so. He was probably heading for somewhere, and when the car got dished, the natural instinct would be to keep going in the same direction."

"But would he stay on the road? Wouldn't he think that if he stayed on the road we would overtake him and see him?"

"Not necessarily. He probably did not think he would be followed as far as this. He couldn't tell that we were after him with another car. Remember he took the only car in sight at the time. He probably thought he had thrown us off long before this."

"All right then." Bond was impatient with the talking. "If he's down the road, we'll find him."

He set off along the road. In places his feet sank in so that the snow came up to just below his knees. It was more like climbing than walking. James Wilson was just behind him. Every step was a laborious exercise, and it was clear that they were not going to make much progress.

The snow was still swirling around them so thickly that it was impossible to see more than a yard or two. Bond was walking with his gun held firmly at the ready, pointing ahead through the snow. James Wilson suddenly struggled to catch him up. He tugged at his arm.

"Is that thing still loaded?" he asked him.

"Of course it is." Bond shook his arm free, and went straight on without looking round.

"You'd better be careful what you do with that. I think you'd better unload it."

"Are you daft? What do you think I brought it for?" His voice was sullen and threatening.

Plodding through the snow, James Wilson would have bet any odds against their catching or seeing the man they were looking for. But if they found him now, if by some freak of chance they suddenly happened on him now, he would only be a couple of yards away by the time they saw him. He would just be a white-coated shape in the midst of the swirling whiteness all around. At five or six yards away he would be as hard to see as Bond was hard to see. If they found him, if they suddenly saw him, he would only be a couple of yards away. A shotgun at a couple of yards. James Wilson tried to push the thought away. He had seen it happen once, in an accident. When you have seen the mess a shotgun can make of a man at close range, you are not in any hurry to see it happen again.

He reached forward and grabbed Bond by the arm again.

"You don't need that loaded," he said. "We can't see him until we're right on top of him."

Bond swung round quickly, bringing the gun round with him.

"Leave me alone," he said fiercely. "This is my business."

James Wilson kept the grip firmly on Bond's arm.

"It's my business too," he said steadily. He felt that the time had come for Bond to be cooled down a bit.

Bond hunched up his shoulders and leaned forward threateningly.

"You keep out of it," he said. "I know what I'm doing and nobody's going to stop me."

The snowflakes came whirling between their faces as they stood there looking at each other. Bond was the taller by a couple of inches. He was very big and very powerfully built. James Wilson could see that he would take plenty of handling if it came to any trouble. But at that moment he was not thinking of the practical, physical trouble of handling Bond. He was thinking of the other thing that suddenly stared him in the face. Bond wanted to kill. It was not simply that be was hotted up and could not cool down yet. Coldly and determinedly, he wanted to kill.

Bond snatched his arm away, and James Wilson let it go. With a scowl Bond turned and set off again through the snow. James Wilson followed. He kept close behind. He kept very close, within grasping distance, as he followed Bond and tried to make up his mind.

He could see, from the way Bond looked and sounded, that he would not unload or drop that gun without being actually forced to. And force, in the mood Bond was in, would mean something more than words, something very much more. It would mean, in effect, that their chase and their search would come to an end while they fought together in the snow. James Wilson knew that he could get the gun away easily. From where he was, from behind, he could put on a double arm lock that would make Bond drop the gun as if it were a red-hot poker. But then what? That would only be the beginning, James Wilson told himself. If you don't muff the arm lock, he drops the gun, and you both go down in the snow, with him in your arms as helpless as a baby. And then what? You're both half buried in the snow, and he can't move, so it's up to you. What do you do next? Stay there, hanging on, keeping him out of trouble? Oh sure, till the morning, till the snow stops, till the summer comes. All right, then, but what is it going to be? Rabbit him with your forehead on the back of his neck, and put him to sleep for a while? And then what? Hang around till he wakes up, and then start scrapping in real earnest? Or clear off and leave him lying in the snow? That's an idea, that last one. It's right in the fashion. This killing instinct is getting infectious. Leave him to freeze to death. Kill him, to stop him from killing the other one. The more the merrier.

James Wilson plodded along close behind Bond, and wished he could make up his mind to something sensible. There were several different reasons why it would be foolish to start any trouble with Bond. For one thing, he might need Bond before this search was over. It looked as if two would be better than one before this thing was finished. And anyway, the job was to find the man he was looking for, not to stop on the way and start scrapping with someone else. He might be mistaken about Bond. Because a man carried a gun, it did not follow that he was going to shoot anyone in cold blood. After all, the man they were looking for was a murderer, and probably lunatic, and a gun was not a bad thing to have on your side.

Not that it's going to make any difference either way, James Wilson thought. Nobody's going to find anybody in this blinding wilderness. His tracks are covered, and we are probably off the trail altogether.

This may be the sensible direction to be looking in, but if the fellow's a lunatic, that cancels things out. The best thing we could do would be to follow our own tracks back to the car and shelter there and hope for a clue in the morning.

It was James Wilson who saw it first. They had been plodding along for the best part of an hour, keeping to the roadway, but seeing no tracks in the thick fresh-fallen snow. It was hard and tiring, wet and cold, and he was just thinking of insisting on going back to the car to wait till morning, before they got lost, before their own tracks disappeared behind them. And then he saw it, a sudden twinkle of light, ahead of them, and seemingly high up in the air.

He called forward to Bond.

"Did you see that?"

Bond stopped.

"See what?" he asked. His eyes had been down on the surface of the snow, still looking for tracks, and he had not seen the light. It had only twinkled for a second or two, and now it was gone.

"I saw a light, up there somewhere." James Wilson pointed ahead. There was nothing to be seen now, but as he looked he realised that the snowflakes were thinner in the air now, they were no longer swirling in a thick white wall around them. The blankness was suddenly lifted away, and they could see quite a distance through the darkness that was lightened by the whiteness of the ground.

"I can't see it," Bond said. They both stood peering forward. There was nothing but the darkness and the whiteness. James Wilson began to wonder if his eyes had fooled him.

Then it came again. They both saw it this time. It was tiny, very high up. It stayed this time for a good ten seconds, and then it was gone again.

"What is it?" Bond asked.

"Might be anything. Probably a light from a house."

"But it seemed to be right up in the air."

"Yes. If it's from a house, there must be a very steep hill in front of us."

"How far away do you think it was?"

"I don't know. It's very difficult to judge. You can see a light from a terrific distance."

"We'd better try to make straight in the direction it came from."

"It may be nothing to do with what we're looking for," James Wilson said. But even as he said it, he could feel that flickering sign of life drawing him like a magnet. "We'll find out, anyway," he said.

But they soon found out that it was not going to be so easy. The direction of the light was not the direction of the road. To make straight for where the light had been, they had to branch off slantingly to the left. Without knowing how far away the light had been, the only chance of finding it was to try to make a straight line towards it. The snow would help them to do that, because once they had started in the right direction they could keep checking that their own footprints were making a straight line behind them. But as soon as they started, they knew it was not going to be so easy. The ground fell away from the road on that side, and the scoop of the ground had caught the drifting snow. Bond was still in front as they started. He had not taken more than half a dozen steps when his foot and his leg went sinking right in, so deeply that it pulled him off his balance, and he fell forward into the drift. His own white shape sank into the whiteness of the snow, and for a moment it seemed as if he had completely disappeared from view. He shouted and struggled and floundered, his whole body sinking deeper in with every movement he tried to make. James Wilson had just checked himself in time to prevent himself from falling into the drift as well. His own feet were down about eight inches in the snow, but beneath them was the hard supporting surface of the edge of the roadway. As he looked at Bond, struggling in the drift, for a moment he had to fight with an almost uncontrollable desire to laugh. Then he shouted to Bond to stop struggling. He could see that he was only sinking deeper and deeper in.

"Give me your hand," he said.

Bond's hand came groping wildly upwards. He leaned forward, but he could not reach it without leaning too far forward and risking being pulled off his balance. Then he saw that Bond's other hand was still holding on to the gun.

"Hold up the gun for me to get hold of," he said.

Bond passed the gun into his right hand, and held it up. The two barrels came pointing straight up at James Wilson. He leaned quickly to one side, so that they pointed past him.

"I'll have the other end, please," he said sourly.

Bond wriggled the gun round in his hand, and held the butt end up. James Wilson took hold of it and tugged firmly and steadily. After a lot of heaving and slipping, Bond managed to clamber back on to the edge of the road. He stood there, leaning forward, gasping and blowing to get his breath back.

"We'll have to pick a better way than that," he muttered.

James Wilson suddenly realised that he was standing with the gun in his hand. For the moment, Bond seemed to have forgotten it. He was not watching him. James Wilson felt with his thumb along the top of the stock, and found the catch and pressed it sideways. The barrels dropped downwards into his other hand, prizing the two cartridges out. He threw them quickly away into the snow, and clicked the gun shut again as quietly as he could. He was sure Bond had not noticed. Bond suddenly remembered about the gun, and turned round and took it out of his hand, almost snatching it, without saying a word.

He'll be mad all right when he finds that out, James Wilson thought. Not that it will make much difference. He is sure to have plenty more in his pockets. And why you keep bothering about that is a mystery. Are you getting the jitters? A farmer carries a gun the way a stockbroker carries an umbrella. There's nothing to it.

They set off plodding again along the road. They both felt it was hopeless trying to slant off in the direction the light had been. If the light had come from a house, then the road would probably lead them round to it. The road had to lead to somewhere.

They had laboured on for about another quarter of a mile when James Wilson suddenly stopped. He called to Bond. But this time he called quietly. Bond turned to see what he wanted.

"Look over there," James Wilson said, and pointed.

Bond looked.

"I can't see anything," he said.

"Yes. That little black patch. Can't you see it?"

Bond strained his eyes in the direction James Wilson was pointing.

"I can see something, yes. What is it?"

"It's a little patch of roof by a chimney. The heat has melted the snow away."

"Are you sure? I can't see as well as that from here."

"Of course I'm sure. I can see the vague outline of the shape of the roof."

It was all just a whiteness against other whiteness, but he thought he could see.

"It's away from the road," Bond said. "Shall we try and go straight across towards it?"

"No. There's sure to be a track or a lane leading off to it, a bit further down the road. If we can find it, that will probably be the easier way. There's no point in landing in a drift if we can help it."

They went on along the road. James Wilson could feel himself ten times as alert as he had been a few minutes before. This was the first house along all the snowy desolate way they had come. It might be the place that the fugitive was making for. There was no real reason for thinking it was, but it might be. And anyway, if the man they were after had been driven to look for shelter, after his car had got ditched, this first house was a very likely place for him to look for it.

They found a narrow track leading off the road towards the house. They turned along it. The outlines of a couple of barns showed that they were coming to a farmhouse. On the track, the snow seemed deeper than on the road. It was all they could do to make any progress through it.

As they neared the house, James Wilson laid a hand on Bond's arm.

"Go carefully," he said.

Bond did not answer. He just went on making his way towards the house. He was gripping his gun and pointing it forward as if he were looking for rats in a barn. As he watched him, James Wilson felt very glad about the cartridges.

They came to the door of the farmhouse. There was a porch jutting out over the door, and the snow suddenly thinned underneath its shelter. As they stood and knocked on the door, for the first time since they had left the car there was no snow round their ankles.

James Wilson had rapped on the door with his fist, but that was not enough for Bond. He knocked with the butt of his gun, as if to bully someone into opening it quickly. The hard, sharp sound seemed to shatter through the darkness.

They heard the sound of an inner door opening, and footsteps crossing a hall. James Wilson felt himself getting taut and ready. The latch of the front door clattered, and the door was pulled open.

There was no light in the hall. But the whiteness threw up from the snow, and they could see a girl standing there.

She was dressed in a heavy tweed skirt and a neat woollen jumper. As she stood there in the doorway, James Wilson could see her face by the white lightness of the snow. He could see the smooth, well-moulded outlines, and the calm, serene expression.

"Yes? Who is it?" Her voice was unhurried and almost casual. It showed not the slightest surprise at the fact that anyone should have struggled through all that snow to make a call. It was a low, liquid, very attractive voice.

James Wilson lifted a snow-laden arm and touched his snow-weighted hat.

"Good evening," he said. "We were—looking for someone. Has anyone come here during the last hour or so?"

She shook her head slowly.

"No. No one. It is hardly an evening to be out, is it? The snow must be very thick."

Bond butted in crudely and roughly.

"We're looking for a murderer. And we think he may have come here to hide. Have you seen him?"

She turned her head slightly towards him.

"But I told you . . . no one has come here."

"He might have done. He must have gone somewhere. How do we know you're telling the truth. Who else is here?" Bond's voice was rasping and impatient.

James Wilson felt a curious resentment inside him as he heard Bond's bullying tone. He knew that he could not really blame him. He knew that it was right. He knew that the enquiry had got to be pushed, and that he ought to be pushing it himself. But he felt a strange resentment at hearing this girl spoken to like that.

The girl had pulled the door open wider. It was fully open now, and she was standing to one side.

"Please come in and satisfy yourselves," she said.

Bond lumbered past her into the hall. He was still holding his gun at the ready. He turned his head quickly each way inside the door. James Wilson hesitated in the porch for a moment. He knew that it was his job to make sure, but he felt himself hesitating in spite of it. He took off his hat as he stepped forward slowly and awkwardly.

"Thank you," he murmured.

She closed the door behind them. It was pitch dark in the hall. James Wilson could feel that the floor was of stone, and he started to knock some of the snow from his clothes, so that he would not make too much mess when he got further into the house. He could not see anything at all, but he felt the girl touch against him as she moved across the hall to open another door. She opened the door into a room that was dancing to the flickering light of a fire.

"Please come in," she said.

They followed her into the room. A big fire was blazing in the grate, throwing sudden flashes of yellow light across the room. There was no other light but the fire.

James Wilson told her who he was. Then he said: "We were following a man in a car. His car skidded into the ditch about a mile or so up the road from here. He must have gone on on foot. We could not find any footprints because most of the snow had fallen since then. We think he probably came somewhere in this direction."

"Oh," she said. She did not sound very interested.

He said: "You haven't heard or seen anything unusual during the last hour or so? You've been indoors all the time, I suppose?"

"I've been indoors, yes. I have been sitting here listening to the radio. I haven't heard anything unusual at all. Why should I? I told you no one had been here."

The flames were dying in the fire, leaving only a red glow, so that the room was getting darker. James Wilson wondered why she did not light a light. He could understand the passage being dark, and there was nothing unusual in sitting by the firelight listening to the radio, but it seemed a bit queer her standing talking to them like this without putting any light on at all.

He was feeling wet and cold, and was beginning to shiver. Almost instinctively he moved across the room to stand nearer to the fire. Bond had stayed over by the door. He had deliberately left the door open, and was listening for any sound out in the passage. He had said nothing since they had come into the house.

She said, quite casually: "Did you say you were looking for a—murderer?"

"Yes," James Wilson answered her. It was funny about this not having any light, he was thinking. The flames have gone out of the fire, and it is practically pitch in this room now. Is she doing this on purpose? Is there something to hide in here? He himself was listening very hard now, listening out into the passage and all over the house.

She was speaking again now. Her voice is nice to listen to, he thought. Where have I ever heard such a pleasant voice? It is so calm, and the pitch is just right.

"Who did he murder?" she was asking.

The answer came in a broken croak from Bond.

"He tried to kill my little girl the way he killed Bennett's."

The sound that came from her was very tiny, very quick. James Wilson jerked his head quickly towards her, but he could not see well enough by the dim glow of the fire. He was not sure, but he almost was. He threw a question at her, any question, just to make her speak again before she had time to recover.

"How long have you lived here?" He spoke abruptly, urgently, so that she would have to answer quickly.

"Oh, quite a long time," she said.

James Wilson's eyes were trying hard to probe through the dim light, but he could not really see. He felt sure of it now. Her voice had tightened. She had answered his question without hesitation, but her words and her tone had been different, they had been consciously controlled. So you were right, he told himself. She did catch her breath when Bond came blurting out about his being the kid's father. She was perfectly calm and collected about having a murderer knocking about in the district, but as soon as Bond says that, she takes it like a kick in the teeth. Does that fit all right? Remember there's no point in letting your mind go chasing off after your own imagination. That could be an ordinary bit of emotion, couldn't it? Well, yes, it could. She is a woman, and hearing that one of the kids was his, it might have been a sudden spurt of sympathy. Keep your feet on the ground, now. Ordinary sympathy, that's all it was. It's funny about this keeping the place dark, all the same. That isn't exactly ordinary.

Then Bond spoke again. The words rushed out of him, as if they had been bottled up inside him and the cork had suddenly popped.

"There's something wrong here! Why is it all dark? Why don't you put the light on? You've got him hiding here!"

James Wilson heard the danger in his voice, the fiercely pent-up misery. He started to move towards Bond, just in case. The girl answered quickly.

"Oh, I'm so sorry. How silly of me to keep you standing here in the dark. I wasn't thinking." She turned her head towards James Wilson. "There's a lamp on the mantelpiece, and matches. Would you like to light it?"

He turned and peered at the top of the mantelpiece, and picked up the box of matches and lighted one. He saw a glass oil lamp with a tall glass chimney, and he lifted the chimney off and held the match to the wick, and as the flame started to run round the circle of the wick he put the chimney on again. It was a long time since he had used an oil lamp, and he vaguely remembered that you had to turn the flame low until the chimney had warmed up. He turned it low, so that the room was still only quarter-lighted. His back was to the room while he was fiddling with the lamp, but he was not caring because he knew that there was no one else in the room except the three of them. The flames from the fire, when they had first come in, had been enough to show the simple furnishing of the room and the lack of anywhere to hide. And if there was anyone hiding in the house, the girl would not be such a fool as to bring them straight into the room where he was. Not that he thought anyone was hiding in the house at all. He gave himself a mental nudge. There was no real reason for suspecting that this girl had anything to do with anything. It was just that this was the first house they had come to. It was just that Bond's demented misery was making everything seem suspicious.

He turned towards Bond. The lamp was still low, and giving little light.

"I think we'd better get going and continue our search outside," he said to him.

Bond almost snarled across the room.

"I'm going to search the house!" he said. "There's something wrong here. She knows more than she's telling."

There was silence in the room for a moment. Then the girl said: "Please search the house. I would rather you did. Then you will know that there is no one else here."

James Wilson turned back to the lamp, and gave the wick screw a little half-twist. He still did not turn it all the way up, for fear of cracking the chimney. He was listening hard all the time now. Never mind what you think or don't think, he was telling himself. There's no point in taking silly chances. If there was anyone hiding here, then to get us both looking upstairs would be the way to give the fellow a chance of getting through the hall and out of the door. So far, nobody has gone out of any door, or else I'm not the listener I used to be. But if we are going to search, then one of us is going to stay where he can hear the hall. Bond can go up, if he wants to. I'll stay put. He won't find anyone. I'd lay any odds on that. She's not the kind to pull a silly feeble bluff of that kind. All the same, I'm glad about those cartridges. He hasn't found out about them yet. I'll feel a lot happier with him going upstairs with an unloaded gun.

He said to Bond: "If you think it's necessary, you take a look over the house. I'll wait for you here."

Bond swung round towards the door into the passage. He'll smash a few things with that gun before he's finished, James Wilson thought.

Bond took a couple of steps towards the passage, and then turned back again into the room.

"I can't search without any lights," he complained. "How can I see anything when it's pitch dark everywhere?"

Again the girl answered quickly and apologetically. "Of course you can't. How thoughtless of me. I'll get you a carrying lantern."

She started to walk towards the door. She walked straight towards it, seeming to ignore the fact that Bond was standing in the opening, right in her way. She took no notice of his being there at all, and it looked as if she would have walked right into him if he had not quickly stepped aside to let her pass. She went out through the doorway, and turned to the right and walked along the passage, walking surely and firmly through the darkness of the passage. They heard her opening a cupboard door in the darkness at the end of the passage, and almost instantly she was closing it again, without any time for groping to find the lantern in the dark. She came straight back, into the room, carrying the lantern in her hand. She knew exactly where it was, James Wilson was thinking. She opened that cupboard in the dark without any fumbling. It is quite black along there, and most people would have fumbled a tiny bit, no matter how well they knew the house. She must have cat's eyes.

She carried the lantern back into the room.

"Here you are," she said. But instead of holding it out for Bond to take, she walked straight past him, across to a table at the other side of the room, and stood the lantern down on the table. Then she went and sat down in a small armchair near the fire.

Bond walked over to the table, pulling a box of matches from his pocket. It was a hurricane lamp, and he instinctively picked it up by the base and shook it gently, listening for the swish of oil inside it.

Then he snapped the catch aside and bent the top back on its hinge and put a match to the wicks. He was well used to lamps, and he knew that the type was fitted with fireproof glass. He turned the flame up full straight away, without waiting for it to warm. Then he snapped the top down again, picked the lantern up in one hand, gun in the other, and strode out of the room.

James Wilson turned to the mantelpiece, and put the other lamp up to its full light. He could hear Bond clumping along the passage and going up the stairs. He looked at the girl. She was sitting in the chair, rather stiffly, looking towards the fire.

He said: "I hope you'll forgive this."

"Forgive what? You have done nothing." She did not look at him when she spoke.

He was conscious of a wish to excuse himself to her. She was reserved, aloof, not even looking towards him when she spoke. He knew he could not blame her. There was no particular reason why she should be warm and friendly. Yet he felt himself wishing she would be. He felt himself wanting to say something nice to her.

"It's rather different with him," he said, jerking his head up towards the clumping sounds that were coming from the floor above. "I suppose I'm used to it. It's just part of my job. But it's different with him. Being the kid's father, I mean."

"Yes. It must be terrible for him." Her voice was very tight as she spoke. He could still hear the natural deep softness of it, but the words were unnaturally tensed and taut. She still did not look towards him.

The warmth of the fire was rapidly melting the snow off his shoes and off his clothes. It was dripping down and making a big wet patch on the fibre matting that covered the floor.

"I'm afraid we are making rather a mess of your house," he said. "We brought an awful lot of snow in with us."

"Please don't worry," she said. "It doesn't matter at all. Really."

She is very taut, he was thinking. There is a definite change since we first arrived. She was calm and composed at first, but now she has gone much tauter. She did not turn a hair when she heard we were looking for a murderer. It was not until Bond said about it being his kid that something seemed to happen to her. You put it down as emotional sentiment, and you may have been right, you probably were. But it could be something else. It just possibly could be something else. It might be that she had prepared herself before we arrived, that she had carefully poised herself to appear calm and unconcerned so as to hide something, and that she is not managing to keep the show going. It might be that. Or it might be that she really was pulling a silly bluff when she challenged Bond to go and look upstairs. Keep listening, he told himself. Keep on your toes. It's a good thing about those cartridges. Whatever happens, it must not happen like that. But I still think you are chasing your own mind round in circles, all the same. I still think it is just emotional sentiment that has made her go like this.

He tried to ease the strange tenseness that seemed to be hanging across the room. He forced a little laugh.

"I hope he doesn't knock the ornaments over with that clumsy gun of his," he said.

"Gun? Has he got a gun?" She was suddenly tauter than ever. But still she did not look.

James Wilson puckered his eyes and looked sharply down at her, hardly believing what he had heard. Had Bond got a gun? The most obvious thing about Bond was that clumsy great thing swishing round and pointing in all directions. He looked down at her hard. What did she mean? he was wondering. What was the point of pretending that she had not noticed it?

"Why has he got a gun?" she went on. Her voice had sunk almost to a whisper. He could hear the strain inside her vibrating her words. "Why has he got a gun? Is he going to . . . shoot somebody?"

There was something very like fear coming out of her now. But he was hardly noticing. He was looking at her and kicking himself. For the time being everything else was pushed away by the thought of what a blind fool he had been. By golly, he thought, by golly James Wilson, you want to get yourself another job pretty quick if that's the way you notice things, if that's the extent of your observation powers. It stuck out a mile all the time, to anyone but you. That was why the room was dark and she forgot to put the light on. That was why she nearly walked into Bond at the doorway. That was why she did not hand the lantern to Bond, but took it over to the table. She knew exactly where the table was, but she did not know just where he was because he was standing still and not talking. By golly.

He heard Bond coming down the stairs and along the passage towards the room. He moved quickly across towards the door, to meet Bond as he came. Bond came clumping in with the lantern and the gun. He stopped short as he saw James Wilson standing in the middle of the room making signs to him.

"What're you doing?" he asked gruffly.

James Wilson did it again. He pointed to his eyes, then pointed behind him to where the girl was sitting, then passed his hand in front of his eyes again.

Bond queried with his face.

"What the devil are you getting at?" he asked.

James Wilson cursed him under his breath, and went up to him and put his mouth close to Bond's ear. "She's blind," he whispered.

Bond looked at him as if to make sure that he meant what he said. Then he looked across to where the girl was sitting. He turned back to James Wilson and spoke as if he was not interested in the news about the girl.

"There's nobody upstairs," he said.

"I didn't think there would be," James Wilson said. "We'd better move on. We've made enough mess in this house."

Bond stood the hurricane lantern down on the floor. He left it burning.

"There's nobody upstairs," he said again, slowly. "But there are signs that somebody else has *been* upstairs."

James Wilson swung round on him quickly.

"What do you mean?"

He did not wait for an answer. He bent down and picked up the hurricane lamp. He went straight through the door and along the passage and up the stairs. The wire struts of the lantern threw an eerie dancing pattern on the walls. There were only three doors opening off the landing. He went into the first one. It was a plainly furnished room, a bedroom, but the bed was not made up and the room did not look as if it were used. He went into the second room. It was neat and tidy, with the bed made ready. A girl's nightdress lay folded on the pillow. This is her room, he thought. His job had taken him prying into plenty of empty bedrooms, and he thought he did not care. But this was her room, her room, and he had a strange feeling that he did not want to pry here. He turned abruptly and went back on to the landing, and into the third room. This one was a contrast. The bed was smoothed and neat, but the rest of the room was out of place and jumbled. The cupboard door was open, and some of the clothes were lying on the floor. They were men's clothes, old and rough like the clothing of a farming labourer. James Wilson walked round the room, looking at it carefully. He wondered if Bond had made this muddle, tumbling the clothes about as he searched. There was nothing that struck him particularly. He went out of the room again, to go downstairs and ask Bond what it was he had seen.

Bond and the girl were both exactly where he had left them. Bond was standing staring fixedly across the room at her. She was still looking towards the fire.

"What did you find upstairs, then?" James Wilson asked him quietly.

Bond kept his eyes fixed on the girl, as if he half-expected her to try to dash out of the room to escape from him at any moment. When he spoke, his voice was challenging and threatening.

"There's a man's clothes up there," he said. "She said she lived here all alone, and yet one of the rooms upstairs is full of a man's clothes."

James Wilson gaped at him.

"But . . . is that what you meant when you said you had found something up there?"

"Isn't that enough?" Bond demanded. "Isn't that enough to show that she isn't telling the truth? Isn't that enough to show that she's hiding something?"

James Wilson frowned at him. He wondered what Bond was usually like. He wondered how much of it could be put down to the shock of having his daughter attacked.

He answered Bond sharply.

"She didn't say that," he told him. "She said there was no one else here with her now, that's all. She said nothing about living alone."

Bond rounded on him fiercely.

"You're on her side," he said. "You know she's trying to hide something, but you're taking her side!"

James Wilson pressed his lips together, to stop himself from saying the kind of words that were trying to come out. He heard the girl's voice across the room, and he saw that she had turned her face towards them.

"Please," she said, softly protesting. "I didn't say I lived here alone. I don't. I said there was no one else in the house now, that's all."

"Who else lives here, then?" Bond threw the question rudely across at her.

"My brother. My brother and I live here together."

"Where is he now, then?"

"He's . . . he's not here. He's away. Away for a few days."

"Away where?" Bond was asking the questions quickly and curtly, using a tone that was making something begin to boil up inside James Wilson.

"Shut up, Bond," he said. He felt the need for steadying his voice.

"You're taking her side!" Bond was beginning to shout now. "Why doesn't she tell us where her brother is?"

The girl got up from her chair and stood facing towards them.

"But I told you . . . he's away for a few days."

"Away where?"

"He's gone over to a farm about ten miles away."

"Ten miles? That doesn't take a few days."

"But he's staying there."

"What for?"

"They are selling up a big farm. He is hoping to buy some machinery."

"When did he go?"

James Wilson put his hand across and took hold of Bond's arm. He was having to fight himself hard now to keep under control. He could not have counted the times when he himself had thrown quickfire bullying questions at random to try and trip someone out, or even just to try and get his own mind into thinking. It was one of those things you did in your stride. You did it and you didn't care. But not with her. Somehow, not with her. He did not like it and he was not going to have it.

"Shut up!" he told Bond again.

"I won't shut up!" Bond shouted. "I'm going to find the man who tried to kill my Dorothy. I'm going to find him. I'm going to find him!"

James Wilson gripped Bond's arm tightly. He could feel that Bond's whole body was trembling. He began to wonder whether the thing had turned the man's mind. Once more he felt glad about the gun, about the cartridges.

"We've got to look for him," he said to Bond. "We've got to look for him somewhere else. He isn't here. You've seen for yourself that he isn't here." He was gripping Bond's arm tightly, trying to put some stiffening into him.

Bond shook his arm and jerked it free.

"She's hiding something," he said. His voice was savage and throaty.

"She's been behaving funnily ever since we first came to the door. There's something queer about the way she acts. It means she's hiding something."

"Pull yourself together!" James Wilson said. "Come on. We're getting out of here."

"She's hiding something," Bond said again. "Why does she act so queerly if she isn't hiding something?"

James Wilson leaned over to him and tried to get close enough to whisper. He did not want to have to say it out loud.

"I told you she was blind, you fool."

Bond suddenly stepped across the room towards the girl. She stood very still, very straight, but she dropped her face a little.

"I'm not so sure," he said. "That may just be part of the trick."

James Wilson felt the nerves inside him starting to tingle. Bond's back was towards him now. He looked at the back of the man and had to hold himself in check.

The girl said nothing. She stood there, her face lowered, knowing that Bond was close to her.

"You knew there was thick snow outside when you came to the door," Bond said.

She did not answer. James Wilson was standing very still. He did not trust himself.

"You did not blunder or feel your way at all when you went to get that lamp," Bond was saying.

Still she did not move or speak. James Wilson took a couple of steps across the room towards them. He was trying very hard to hold himself.

"How do we know that's not just part of the trick?" Bond said again.

He suddenly passed his hand quickly in front of her eyes. James Wilson took another step forward. He was moving unconsciously. His nerves were tingling and his head was starting to press inside.

Bond drew his hand back. He was standing in front of her, looking at her disbelievingly. He suddenly thought of a better test. Holding his hand well away from her face, he swished it quickly towards her in a slapping movement, to see if she flinched. He did not hit her. His hand stopped an inch or two short of her face.

James Wilson felt his fists bunching up and he did not try to stop them. He took another step forward, and grabbed Bond by the shoulder and swung him round. He did not care about anything except that it was her and it could not happen, it could not go on happening and he had to stop it the quickest way. As Bond came swinging round, James Wilson hit him. He hit him on the side of the jaw. He knew how to hit, and he did it right and he did it very hard.

The shotgun went clattering down into the hearth as Bond's hand lost the power to hold it. There had been no mistakes in that punch. The muscles in Bond's legs ceased to be of any use. He sagged down on to the floor as if his legs had been made of plasticine.

The girl had taken a quick step backwards. Now she was standing close to the wall, backing against it, touching it for safety.

James Wilson looked down at the crumpled figure of Bond on the floor. His fist was still bunched up tight. The deep, fierce hatred of Bond's behaviour to the girl was still burning inside him. He looked at the motionless body on the floor, and then lifted his head towards the girl.

"I'm sorry . . . I'm sorry," he said, "I'm terribly sorry."

She shook her head.

"No," she said. "Please don't be."

"I . . . he . . ." he fumbled for what to say. "Please try to make allowances for him. He is so upset he hardly knows what he is doing."

"It is all right. Please do not apologise." She hesitated, and then: "It was nice of you. I would like to say thank you. It was nice of you."

He felt his cheeks beginning to burn. He took his eyes away from her face. He was looking at Bond again.

He said, abruptly: "I wonder if you'd mind . . . going out of the room for a little while . . . upstairs perhaps." He was looking at Bond.

"Yes. I'd better." She moved away from the wall, and made a detour round the room to avoid Bond. He watched her go. She walked very gracefully. Her hair made him think of a well-groomed Irish setter.

He heard her going up the stairs, and he looked at Bond and wondered what was coming now. The heat of it all had gone out of him, and he looked at Bond and weighed it up and wondered what was coming. He wondered if all he had done was to land himself with a fight on his hands. This was not exactly getting on with the job he was out to do. This was a stroll down a side alley. You somehow thought you were going to tangle with him, he remembered. Back there in the snow, about the gun. You managed to put it aside, back there. It did not seem to matter all that much. And then when you had snaffled the cartridges, it seemed to be all right. But you had

the feeling, even then. No excuses, now. You know what the job is.
When are you going to learn to keep to the high street? Side alley
Wilson. All right. But this was different, I don't care what you say,
what anyone says. This was different and if anyone did that again to
her you'd do it again to him or anyone else. Whatever anyone did to
her they'd get the same from you. By golly, though. You ought to
have counted the minutes. He certainly took it. You haven't lost the
knack with that right arm of yours.

Bond was stirring, and now he was sitting up on the floor and was
feeling his chin with his hand. James Wilson stood a couple of yards
away, just out of reach. He watched him and wondered what was
coming.

Bond raised his head and looked at him. Then he looked to where
the girl had been standing, and then looked slowly all round the
room to find her. When he saw that she was not there he got slowly
to his feet. He bent down and picked up the gun from where it had
fallen in the hearth.

James Wilson watched him steadily. James Wilson's knees were
slightly bent and the weight of his body was carefully balanced on
the balls of his feet. He wondered what was coming.

Bond fingered his chin and looked at him. James Wilson looked
him steadily in his eyes. Then Bond turned his head slowly all round
the room again, as if he was looking for the girl. He took it, James
Wilson thought. I believe he took it.

One of them had to say something. James Wilson thought it might
be easier for him.

"I had to hit you, Bond," he said. "I had to stop you."

Bond was not looking him in the eyes now. When he spoke, his
voice was tired and limp. The bullying had gone from it.

"Where is she?" he asked.

"She has gone."

"Upstairs?"

"Yes."

There was silence for a few moments. Then:

"Did I hit her?"

"No. You didn't hit her."

"Are you sure?"

"Yes. You didn't hit her."

"Did I touch her?"

"No. Not actually."

"I was going to?"

"I don't know. Probably."

"Did I frighten her?"

"I don't know. In a way, I suppose."

"Did she know what I was doing?"

"In a way, I suppose."

"But I didn't hit her? You are sure I didn't hit her?"

"You didn't hit her."

"But I might have touched her?"

"No."

Bond passed his hand slowly across his forehead.

"I didn't know," he said. "I simply didn't know. It was something that had hold of me. I couldn't stop it."

James Wilson did not say anything. He could see how it was.

Bond said: "I've got to find him. That's all it is. That's all. I've got to find him. I've got to."

James Wilson saw that his hands were beginning to firm themselves on to the gun. He knew that it was not over. A spasm was ended, but the whole thing was not over.

He said: "We'll find him, Bond. I promise you. We'll find him."

"I've got to find him. I swear to God I'll find him."

"We'll find him, Bond."

"Let's go. We mustn't waste time."

James Wilson shuddered a little at the thought of the night outside.

"I'll try and find out about the district from her," he said. "She'll be able to tell us what other farms or villages there are along the road."

"Yes." Bond hesitated. "I'll wait outside the front door. Do you mind? I mean . . ." he jerked his head in the direction of upstairs. "Will you do it for me?" The sudden humility made him seem like a child.

"Do what?"

"You know. Her. Perhaps you can say something."

"Yes, I will. She understands."

They walked together across the passage and opened the front door. It was snowing heavily again, just as heavily as before. There was nothing outside but the darkness and the solid curtain of the white flakes drifting down.

"We're not going to do much finding in this," he muttered.

"We must. We've got to find him."

"You wait out here. I'll go back and talk to her. At least we can find out a few places to look."

He closed the front door, leaving Bond in the porch outside. He walked across the passage to the foot of the stairs, and called up them.

"Hullo?" he called.

She answered quickly.

"Yes?"

"May I speak to you?"

"Yes. Please go back into the parlour. I'll be down in half a moment."

He walked back into the room and over to the fire. The wet was creeping through his socks and down inside his collar. The fire was warm and cheerful, and it made the thought of the night outside more unpleasant than ever. You'll have to make a try, he thought, but you know well enough that you haven't got a hope tonight. How could anyone find anything in that? All you can do is to wander around until you both get lost, or until you're so tired with ploughing through the snow that you have to pack it up. You've certainly got yourself into something this time.

He looked at the patches of wet that he and Bond had left on the floor matting. There were little flat slivers of ice still there that had come away from the heels of their shoes. A nice mess to make. There was a big dark patch where Bond had sprawled on the ground. The matting was a kind of neutral colour, and it went dark when it was wet. They had made it all patchy between them. A pretty nice mess. She must be thinking pretty highly of us, he thought. Nice to have callers. Specially when they behave like a couple of mad beasts. Do drop in again any time you are passing, Mr. Wilson. I can just hear her.

She was coming down the stairs now. She paused in the open doorway expectantly. He cleared his throat, and she quickly placed him in the room by the sound, and walked over and sat down in the same armchair again.

He said: "I'm awfully sorry about everything."

"Why? There's nothing you need be sorry about. If you . . ." she corrected herself ". . . if he is satisfied that there is no one hiding here, I suppose you will want to be off continuing your search."

"Yes."

"It's an unpleasant night to have to be doing that sort of thing, isn't it?"

"Yes. Bond—that's his name—wanted me to tell you that he was sorry about what happened."

"Please. There is no need to talk about it."

"He got sort of pent-up. He's taken it pretty hard you know. I mean about that kid of his. He didn't mean to behave like that."

"There was nothing to apologise about. I know he must feel dreadful."

"He is waiting outside, in the porch."

"Yes, I heard him go out."

We are a bit lost here, and it's hard to see much tonight. I wondered if you could tell us anything about the district." He had said it before he realised what a clumsy question it was to ask her. For a moment he felt as if he was behaving almost as badly as Bond. He was grateful when she took it and answered without any embarrassment or awkwardness.

"You came up the long climbing road from Selton, didn't you?"

"Yes."

"And then dropped slightly down again before you got here."

"Yes. It was on the down slope that we ditched the car."

"You turned left off the road to come along here to the house."

"Yes."

"If you keep on along the road, in less than a quarter of a mile it forks into two. The left one still climbs upwards, but not very steeply. It is narrow, and really just a loop off the other one. It passes two farms, and then winds round and joins the other road again. If you take the right fork, you come to the village in a little over half a mile."

"Is it much of a village?"

"Very small. A few cottages, a little general store, and a small inn."

"It is pretty lonely round here, then."

"It is lonely, yes. We are right up on the moors here. There are not many people about. More in the summer, of course."

He thought for a moment. He was getting his bearings, and thinking of the flicker of light that he and Bond had seen, high up somewhere.

He pointed his arm across the room in the direction of the front of the house.

"Does the left fork go up that hill there?"

"Which way?" she asked.

He dropped his arm and wished he could stop being such a clumsy fool.

"Directly in front of the house. There must be a steep hill there. Which road goes up to it?"

"There is no road up there."

"But there is a hill? There must be a hill there."

"There is a hill opposite the house, yes. But it is simply moorland. There is no road up to it."

"Is there no house up there? No farm?"

"No. Nothing at all."

"Are you sure?"

"Yes. Quite sure. What makes you think there ought to be a farm up there?"

"Not a farm specially. But something."

"There isn't. What makes you think there is?"

"We saw a light up there."

"You saw—what?"

"We saw a light up there."

She shook her head quickly.

"No. You couldn't have done. Not up there. There is nothing."

"We saw a light all right. I noted the direction very carefully."

"When did you see it? When did you think you saw it? Where from?"

"From back along the road. Just after we had left the car."

"But you probably couldn't be sure of the direction from there."

"Why not?"

"It must be quite easy to make a mistake, in the dark and in the snow."

"No. I noted the direction very carefully."

"You must have made a mistake all the same. There is nothing up that hill. Nothing at all. Perhaps the light came from this house. That would have been in the same direction."

"No. The light we saw was high up. Higher than this house."

"If it came from an upstairs window it would look quite high up, wouldn't it?"

"Not high enough. And anyway—did you have a light upstairs a little while before we came?"

She hesitated. It was quite a long pause.

"No," she answered at last.

He was looking at her carefully. One half of him was pulling away, to get outside and get on with the search and get on with the job. The other half was holding him, wanting to go on talking to her, not quite knowing why.

"The snow is pretty thick outside," he said.

"Yes."

"It's one of the heaviest falls I've ever seen."

"We seem to get it up here. We are often snowbound for several days."

"I shouldn't think you're far off being snowbound now."

"And it is still snowing," she said.

"Yes. It stopped just before we arrived here, but it was coming down heavily again when I looked outside just now."

"I know. I can hear it."

"You can hear it?"

"Yes. Can't you?"

"Well—no, not exactly."

"I can. I can always hear snow. It is not so much a sound as a kind of added silence. You ought to try. You can hear fog too, if you practise."

The half of him that wanted to get on with the search was beginning to tug at his conscience. He looked again at the mess of wet patches on the floor.

"I'm sorry we brought so much snow in with us," he said. "Thank you very much for the help you have given."

"I'm afraid it has not been very much." She stood up, knowing that he was about to go.

He asked her suddenly: "You did say that you had not been out of the house for the last hour or two, didn't you?"

"Yes." She answered patiently, as if his reiteration were merely foolish.

His spine was suddenly tingling. His eyes had hardened, and were probing in quick, keen jumps round the room.

He was looking at the dark, damp patches on the matting that covered the floor. He was counting them and placing them. From those dark patches, he could plot the movements of himself and Bond. Wherever they had stood they had left a patch. There was the one around his feet as he stood there now. There was another, farther along by the hearth, where he had stood before. A big blurred one showed where Bond had sprawled on the floor. He was looking at the patches, and counting them and placing them and trying to put them in order. His, where he had first entered, then across and in front of the fire. Bond's, near the door, a big one where he had stood so long, a fainter one against the table where he had stood while he lighted the hurricane lantern. He stood there now, checking them carefully in his mind. Into the room, over towards the fire, along in front of the hearth, across to the door again. Bond, near the door, moving to one side then across to the table where she had stood the lantern down. Out again, in again, then slowly across the room, then the big patch where he had sprawled. James Wilson remembered that Bond had been alone in the room with her while he had gone looking upstairs. But Bond seemed to have been standing rigidly still in the same position all that time. He would not have gone right over there, anyway. Not right over there.

He felt the tingling going up his spine. He glanced at the girl. She was standing with her face towards the fire, waiting for him to go, waiting to hear him move. As he stepped from the fireplace, he watched her. He did not walk towards the door, but went right up to the far end of the room, past the table. He saw her swing round quickly, following his movements in that unexpected direction. She did not say anything.

Now he was looking down at the floor, bending to look at it closely. Against the patch on the floor was an upright wooden chair with wooden arms. He bent down and wiped his finger along one of the arms. He could see that the wood was wet in places, on the seat and in the middle of the back and on top of one of the arms. He walked back into the middle of the room.

"We'd better go on and see if we can find that inn," he said.

"You can't miss the village if you take the right-hand fork."

"Good." He hesitated. Then: "You did say that no one had been here this evening except for us, didn't you?"

"Yes." Her voice was deep and soft. It told him nothing.

He stood for a moment, looking at her. He was wishing that she did not have to lie to him.

FOUR

He walked across to the door and she followed, thinking he was going. He paused at the door of the room and turned to her.

"May I borrow the hurricane lantern before I go?" he asked.

"Before you go?"

"I mean I will bring it back to you before we go right away."

She did not answer.

"Do you mind if I borrow it?" he asked again.

"Of course, by all means."

He thought the tautness had come back into her voice again. He picked up the lantern from where Bond had left it standing on the floor. It was still burning. He walked across the passage towards the front door. She came behind him.

"You are taking it outside?"

"Yes, if I may? I'll bring it back quite soon."

He opened the front door. The light from the lantern threw out on to the thick whirling flakes of snow that were coming down steadily. He stepped out into the porch. Bond wasn't there. He lifted the lantern above his head and he could see Bond's footsteps leading straight away through the snow.

"Bond!" he called.

There was no answer. The girl was standing behind him in the doorway.

"He seems to have gone," he said.

"Gone where? Where has he gone?"

"I don't know."

He cupped his free hand to his mouth and shouted into the snow.

"Bond! Hello! Bond!" There was no answer.

"The fool's gone ramping off again!" he exclaimed.

"Where has he gone?" she asked again.

"Just ploughing his way blindly through the snow," he said. He had used the word before he had realised it. He wished he had not said it, and he turned round towards her, feeling that he wanted to make up for it by saying something nice to her.

"Don't stand by the open door," he said. "You'll only get cold."

"Are you going now?"

"More or less. I'll bring the lantern back very soon. I'll knock on the front door again."

He stepped out a couple of paces into the snow and waited for her to close the door.

When she had closed it he looked with the light of the lantern at Bond's deep footprints leading away, and at the footprints of the two of them coming towards the house. Already those earlier footprints were blurred, so thickly and gustily was the snow falling. He looked at them carefully, trying to find others. He raised and lowered the lantern, getting the light at varying angles across the top of the snow, but he could see no other footprints.

Half an hour of this kind of snow would have been quite enough to hide them, he was thinking. And he may have had an hour.

He went back close to the porch and turned to one side. With deep laborious steps he plodded his way completely round the house, searching ahead of him for marks in the snow. He found nothing. He came back to the porch again. He looked at Bond's fresh footsteps and wondered where he had gone. He did not want to follow Bond on any wild chase through the night. It was possible that Bond had seen something or heard something while he was standing in the porch and had gone after it, but he did not think so. More likely he was just ramping off the way he had done before, just itching mad to catch the man.

James Wilson started to follow Bond's footprints towards the narrow lane. The snow was inches up his legs, and he used the big footprints to make it easier for walking. He was not going to follow Bond, but there was somewhere he knew he had to look. There was no one in the farmhouse, but there had been earlier. Of that he was sure. If the man had come to the farmhouse and had feared that he might be followed, or looked for there, he might be lying low for the night in one of the barns that they had seen as they came along the lane.

James Wilson followed along Bond's footprints until he was level with the low white shapes of the barns. Bond's footprints went straight on towards the road. James Wilson turned towards the barn, peering through the whirling snow. He went blundering and sloushing his way through the thick piled snow and came to a gate. The snow was above the bottom bar. He climbed over the gate. He could see no marks of any kind there. Snow was double-crossing stuff, he was thinking. One minute it could show you everything, and an hour later it could take everything away.

He went across towards the first barn. He found the big double door with the snow piled against it. Through the hasps of the door was a heavy padlock. He tugged at it and found that it was locked. Unless there was another way in, the padlock on the outside meant that there could be no one inside. He struggled his way all round the barn and could see no other way in. Then he went along to the second barn. The doors of this one were closed, but the padlock hung on one hasp only, so that the doors were not locked. He felt his pulses quickening. Remember who you're looking for, he told himself quickly. This isn't any sneak thief. This is a man who has a murder and a try to his credit the last two days.

His pulses were quickening, but not with fear. The man picked children and used his hands. It was not likely that he would be armed. He used his hands and James Wilson could use his too. He took hold of the hasp of the door and pulled at it. The snow was piled up against it, and it would only move an inch. He stood the lantern down on the top of the snow. He stood it carefully behind him so that if anyone came out through the door the light would be behind him and in the other man's eyes. Then he started laboriously to scoop the snow away with his hands to make room for the door to open. It was difficult, slow work without a spade. He had not measured the time, but he reckoned he must have been at it for ten or fifteen minutes by the time he had cleared a long V-shaped piece of ground outside the door. Then he pulled the door slowly open. It was hung close to the ground and at first it came open only about a foot. He could have got in through, but he did not want to take any risk of getting caught in the doorway if anything was happening. He had another go at the snow, scraping the ground clean with his foot, and then managed to get the door open a full yard.

He picked up the lantern again and stepped towards the opening. He waited for several moments just outside, listening carefully. His own breath was the only thing he could hear. Then he held the lantern out at arm's length and pushed it through the opening. Still there was no sound. By the light of the lantern he could look through and see one wheel of a tractor inside the door. Gauging the distance carefully, he suddenly stepped quickly through right clear of the doorway, and swung round quickly.

The flickering light of the shaking lantern was sending shadows darting all over the inside of the barn. He could see the tractor and a plough and a wide raking machine. He listened again. There was no sound in the barn. He held the lantern high in his left hand and walked slowly round inside the wall. He walked sideways, keeping his back to the wall, and his right fist was clenched and his arm was bent and flexed.

The shadows moved as the lantern moved, and every few feet he stopped, holding the lantern as still as he could, watching for any shadow to come to life. He went round the wall and came to the door again. There was no one in there. He went outside the door and cast the light round in a wide circle over the snow. There were no steps leading away from the barn. No one had ducked out while he was looking. He pushed the door shut again and followed his own footprints back to the gate, and then on to the lane and then back towards the house.

He went very slowly back to the house. He was trying to sort the thing out in his mind. He was trying to get the values right, and to stop his ideas from going round in circles. He was not quite sure whether he had found out everything or found out exactly nothing.

Someone had been there earlier in the evening, and she had lied about it. That, in a way, was the only solid thing he knew. And now he was trying to tie that up with the fact that the man they were after had been coming in this direction. You are trying to lean pretty heavily on coincidence, he told himself. You are trying to fit things up the easy way. But are you, though? Are you really? You've got quite a bit of excuse for trying to tie the two things up together. Suppose someone else, someone quite different, came to her house earlier, and she had decided to lie about it. That's all right. She might have fifty different reasons. But then, when you tell her that you are looking for a murderer, and when you show suspicion as clearly as Bond did, you'd think if she had any sense she would stop telling fairy stories in case it got her mixed up in something worse. Although you never know with people, and that is never a good theory to go on. But murder is murder. And whatever else she may be, she is not a fool.

She lied about somebody going there, and she did it very well indeed. She kept up the casual, disinterested stuff all the time. It must have taken some doing. She must have something pretty solid at the back of her, somewhere. And she very nearly did it on you. If you had not gone back into that room, to ask her where the road went to, you would not have noticed anything. Perhaps you should have noticed it before, but you and Bond had splathered so much wet about the house that you could hardly blame yourself for not noticing. It was not very obvious. And so, right up to the very last moment, she had you fooled. And she still thinks she has. Remember she still thinks she has.

But that is only one thing. That is only the fact that someone came to the house earlier on and she denies it. That does not prove that the person who came to the house is the man you are looking for. It does not even start to prove it. And if it were someone quite different, you may spend hours barking up the wrong tree. You'd better sort that question out as quickly as you can, he thought. It should not be difficult. Just let her know that you have seen through it, that you know someone came to the house, that you know she is lying. Put on the heat for a bit. If the person who came to the house was someone quite different, you can soon put the wind up her and make her think that she is getting herself involved in a murder case. If it was someone quite different, then she'll soon come across if you scare her a bit. That should not be difficult. You've scared enough people in your time, you've got the knack all right. That should not be difficult. Oh, no, not a bit. Easy as anything. You can try smacking her in the face, can't you? You can pick up where Bond left off. Come on now. How do you put the pressure on with a girl who is blind? How do you make yourself do it? Tell me that.

He trudged back slowly to the house. The snow was still whirling down in huge flakes, getting thicker and thicker. He stood for several minutes outside the door of the house, thinking and wondering. Then he lifted his hand and knocked on the door.

He heard her coming out of the room and crossing the passage. She pulled the door open.

"Yes?" she asked.

"I've brought your lantern back."

"Oh. Was it—all right?"

"How do you mean, all right? It didn't blow out."

"I mean, did it serve your purpose?"

"It helped me to have a look round, yes."

"Did you find anything?"

"Nothing special."

"Didn't you find where the other man had gone, the one you called Bond?"

"No."

"He's not with you now?"

"No. I don't know where he has gone."

"Do you think he will come back here?"

"I've no idea. I don't know where he has gone."

"He might not come back here," she suggested. "He might have decided not to wait for you. He'll probably go on along the road, and find the village and stay there for the night." She spoke eagerly, as if she hoped to hear him agree with her.

He said: "That's possible. I just don't know where he has gone."

He was still holding the lantern. She had made no move to show that she wanted him to hand it to her.

"Shall I stand the lantern down in the hall?" he asked her.

"Thank you." She moved to the side of the doorway to let him pass.

He stepped just inside the door, and stood the lantern down against the wall. He hesitated for a moment, and then said:

"I wonder if you'd mind—could I just come in and warm my hands for a few minutes before I set off again?"

"Of course!" she exclaimed. She pushed the front door shut. "I should have asked you, but I thought you would not want to spare the time."

She led the way into the sitting-room again. She went over and sat down in her same chair by the fire. He followed her.

"I should take your coat off and dry it a bit," she suggested. "You must be soaked."

"I am a bit wet." He thought, she does not seem in any violent hurry to get rid of me. I can't think why, unless she gets a kick out of bluffing. But it suits me all right.

He took off his coat, shook it gently into the stone hearth, and managed to make it hang on the corner of the mantelpiece.

"Thank you," he said. He held his hands towards the fire and rubbed them together.

"It's a terrible night, a terrible storm," she said.

"It is."

"If it keeps on like this all night, we shall be cut off from the village. It always drifts badly into the valley where the road is."

"You've lived round here a long time?"

"Yes, quite a long time, on and off."

"You seem to know the district well."

"Quite well, yes."

She was sitting with her face towards the fire, and he was looking at the side of her face, at her hair, glinting from good brushing, fiery copper-coloured, and he was thinking how strangely sweet her face was. He felt he did not want to go away from her. Quite apart from the reasons he had for talking to her, for finding something out, he had an extra feeling that he did not want to go away from her. She reminds you of something or someone, he thought. Who is it she reminds you of?

He stood with his back to the fire, holding his hands out behind him to warm them. He looked at her and wondered how to talk to her. He did not want to muck it up.

"You must get quite lonely living right out here," he said.

"Not particularly. I don't notice it much."

That was a pretty clumsy start, he told himself. It was too much like hanging out a hook with a big fat bait on it. That is not the way you want to start talking to her. You do not want to fish so obviously. Remember that she thinks she has fooled you. And remember that her head is screwed on very much all right. You are supposed to have given this house a clean bill, and you are simply in it now because you want to warm yourself and dry yourself a bit. If you start to probe her, she will shut up like a clam, and a clever clam at that. You'll have to try to let things come without pulling at them.

He stood there, warming his hands, not saying anything. It was very quiet in the room, and yet the silence did not feel awkward. It was almost as if they were sharing something. He did not quite know what he meant by that, but it did feel somehow as if they were sharing something.

He did not hurry to break the silence, and in the end it was she who spoke.

"Do you mean that you think you would be lonely if you lived in a place like this?"

"Well, I . . ." He laughed. "Yes—I suppose that's what I meant, really." Who is it she reminds you of? he wondered. It might be someone you've seen on the films, eh? Hepburn? No, not Hepburn. Definitely not Hepburn.

"You have always lived in towns?" she asked.

"More or less." If it wasn't someone on the films, could it be a sculpture you've seen somewhere?

"Towns can be lonely, can't they?"

"I suppose they can," he said, "for some people."

"But not for you?"

He hesitated. The question had never been put into words for him before. She asked it so softly, so earnestly, that he felt a simple one-word answer would be almost the same as ignoring her question altogether. She made him feel as if he wanted to tell her things.

"I don't know," he said slowly. "I'm not sure I have ever thought it out."

"Sometimes the people who are never alone are the loneliest of all."

"Yes." He said it in a way that asked her to go on.

"Don't you think so?" she asked.

"I don't know. I've never thought it out."

"I think you have."

He puckered his eyes and looked at her hard. "What do you mean?"

She smiled, then laughed softly.

"What I say."

"How do you know what I've thought out and what I haven't?"

"I didn't say I knew. I said I think."

"Mind reader?"

She shook her head.

"Not at all."

"But you know whether I've thought that out or not?"

"Mmm. I think you have."

"What makes you think so?"

She waited a moment. When she spoke again her voice was dreamy.

"Because, some time or other, most lonely people have tried to think out about loneliness."

"You mean—you think I'm a lonely person?"

"In some way—yes." She nodded her head slowly.

"What makes you think that?"

"Isn't it so?"

He did not want to answer. He was suddenly thinking about it hard, and he did not want to answer.

"What makes you think so?" he asked again.

She shrugged her shoulders.

"Perhaps it is just that one can sense it in another."

He was looking at her, and the feeling of wanting to tell her things was stronger in him all the time. He wanted to have known her for ages and ages. He wanted to talk to her with all the barriers pushed away. He wanted to ask her to hold some of the things that he had carried alone for so long. He did not know why he felt that way, and he knew it was foolish. But he felt it just the same.

She suddenly stood up from her chair, and held out a hand towards him.

"Let me feel your hands," she said.

He put out a hand, and took hold of hers. She shuddered a little as their hands touched.

"You're absolutely freezing, still." She pulled her hand away. "Put a couple of those split logs on the fire and liven it up a bit, while I go and get you something hot to put inside you."

She turned and walked across the room and through the door. He watched her go, and then, moving almost mechanically, he picked up a log from a basket by the side of the hearth and threw it on the fire, and jabbed it with his foot well down into the glowing embers. The wood was dry, and it filled the room with a cheerful crackling sound. He watched the burst of sparks as the flame came licking up round the new wood. He listened to the sounds the girl was making in the kitchen along the passage. He could hear the clink of crockery. It suddenly crossed his mind how difficult it must be, how clever it was. He walked to the door and called to her along the passage.

"Don't trouble to get me anything, please."

"It isn't any trouble."

"Can I come and help you?"

"No. Please don't. Stay by the fire till I bring it to you. It won't be long."

He went slowly back to the fire. His mind was in a muddle. He was muddled about himself, as well as about her. He did not want to think about himself just now, and he kicked savagely down at the log again, trying to jerk his mind straight. He tried to push the other things out and to think about the job on his hands. She did not seem in any hurry to get rid of him. She did not seem to want him to go. And that does not make sense, he told himself. You must be imagining things. You must be persuading yourself that she likes your company. It does not make sense for her to want you hanging around in the house here. She has something to hide, and she knows who you are, and that means you are just about the last person in the world that she wants hanging around here. She does not want to give herself away by appearing too frantically anxious to get you off the premises, but she cannot want you to stay. That is obvious. But she did not have to offer you a hot drink, did she? Then why did she do it? And she did not have to start that funny kind of talk, and that strange friendly voice, did she? Did she?

It is a pity you have to be against her, he thought suddenly. It's the same old pity. The same old thing it always is. You are on the job, and she is hiding something from you, and that puts you against her and you do not want to be against her. You'd give a lot not to be against her.

He heard her coming along the passage, and he looked towards the door. She came in, carrying a tray. She walked steadily over to the fire with it.

"Would you like to draw that small table up to the fire here?" she said.

He went quickly to the little table and pulled it across to the fireplace. Then he took the tray from her hands and stood it down on the table. She followed the tray down with her hand, checking its position. Then she moved her chair a little nearer to the table.

"Cocoa," she said. "Drink it while it is hot. I always think it is more warming than tea or coffee."

She picked up one of the cups herself and started to sip it.

"That cheese and biscuits is for you," she said. "Help yourself."

"It's awfully kind of you. I don't know how to thank you."

"You make it sound as if it were a banquet."

"Cocoa and cheese at the right moment can be better than any banquet."

"That's the same with most things, isn't it?" she asked.

"It's the same with most things, yes."

"Like if you were hopelessly lost somewhere, and you met a tramp, for a moment he would feel like the best friend you ever had."

James Wilson laughed.

"You seem to be a bit of a philosopher," he said.

She shook her head.

"I wasn't meaning to be."

"This cocoa is jolly good, anyway. At the moment I wouldn't trade it for caviar and vodka."

"That's easy to say. You know you haven't got the chance."

"I'm not so sure. It feels horribly like Russia outside tonight."

She shivered at the thought.

"I'm glad I haven't got to go out," she said.

"Yes. It isn't exactly tempting." As he said it, the thought of going out again into that thick white blizzard, late as this, to clamber blindly through the piled snow for the rest of the night seemed horribly unreal.

"Do you think Bond will come back here?" she asked.

"I don't know at all. I have simply no idea where he has gone to. He might come back any moment. I suppose so. I just don't know."

"I suppose that some time sooner or later he's bound to come back looking for you, isn't he?"

"I don't know."

"But I mean, he wouldn't separate himself from you altogether, would he? I mean you're together, aren't you?"

"Yes, I suppose so, but only more or less by accident."

"By accident?"

"Yes. He hopped into the car just as I was driving off. Otherwise I would have been alone."

"But you know him well?"

"I'd never seen him until yesterday. Why are you asking?"

"I am just interested, that's all."

"Interested in what?"

"In you and him."

He laughed.

"We are not very interesting," he said. I've got it, he thought. I've got it. It's not a sculpture and it's not a film star that she reminds you of. It was a famous painting, and you saw it reproduced in a magazine somewhere.

Her mind was still probing in the same direction. "You've been with him alone for several hours, haven't you?" she persisted.

"Yes. While I tried to push the car through the snowstorm."

"You know something about what he is like then? What kind of a man he is?"

"Why are you asking all this?"

"I don't know. I'm only interested in people."

"I'm afraid you saw him at rather a bad moment," he said. "He was half-batty with misery, poor devil."

He wished he could have the sense to avoid using words like "see" to her.

She sipped her cocoa slowly.

"If he comes back here," she said, "I would like you both to go. I would rather he didn't come in."

"Of course," he said.

Then she said quietly and evenly: "I am frightened of him."

"I am so terribly sorry," he said, thinking he understood what she meant.

"Oh, it's nothing to do with what happened," she said. "Please don't think that. Please don't think I am still worrying about that. It was nothing."

He waited, hoping that she would go on, hoping that she would explain herself in some way. But when she spoke again she seemed to have put Bond out of her mind.

"Are you getting any warmer?"

It was her soft, friendly voice again.

"Much, thank you. This cocoa's marvellous. It was awfully kind of you."

"Would you like some more?"

"No, thank you." He wondered if this was his cue to go. Then he knew that it wasn't, because she said:

"Do smoke if you want to."

He knew that he could not be fooling himself any longer. She was not merely in no hurry to get him out of the house. She seemed actually to be trying to delay his going. As he searched for his cigarettes and found them, he was trying quickly to decide what her reason was most likely to be. Did she know that there was something to be discovered outside, and therefore want to delay him from looking? He did not think that was the answer. She had made no attempt to delay him until Bond had gone. The answer could not be as simple as that. He felt, vaguely but instinctively, that she had some other reason. He tried to test her.

"I'll have to be getting on, I suppose," he said. "I have got work to do."

She nodded her head.

"Yes, but surely it is almost impossible to carry on much search on a night like this, isn't it?"

"It's not exactly easy," he admitted.

"What exactly is your job?" she asked suddenly.

"I thought you knew. I thought I told you."

"You told me that you were connected with the police," she said.

"Well, that's all there is to it."

"I suppose it's very interesting."

He grunted noncommittally.

"Do you like it?"

He hesitated.

"Not always," he said.

Again he had that feeling that he didn't want to fob her off with artificial brevities.

"What don't you like about it?" she asked.

"Sometimes it's not very pleasant."

"You mean, for instance, having to trudge around on a beastly night like this?"

"That wasn't what I meant, no."

"Tell me about some of the times when it hasn't been very pleasant," she said softly.

He felt himself tightening his hands together and he was saying to himself, snap out of this, snap out of this damned silly feeling that you want to unburden your soul to this perfect stranger. Since when have you acquired the habit of letting idle small talk get under your skin and make you want to soften up and tell things? You must be tired. You must need a holiday. You're supposed to be trying to find something out from this girl, and all you're doing is to sit here and want to tell her a lot of soft things that are bottled up inside you.

"You wouldn't be interested," he said lamely. "You wouldn't understand."

"Wouldn't understand?"

Her voice was soft and almost expressionless, and by the very lack of persuasion in its tone, he knew, he thought, that no one he had ever known would understand more easily. He sat there looking at her, holding back the words that tried to come pouring out of him. He wanted to say, "I hate it because it takes me into all the muck that ever happens. Because it forces on me the need to suspect everyone and probe everyone, to dig into the dirt of everyone's mind and everyone's private life. I hate it because it makes me be against people always." But he held the words back.

She had finished her cocoa, and she put the cup back on to the tray, feeling for the place with her little finger before she put it down.

"What will you do," she asked casually, "if you find this person you are looking for?"

"Arrest him. Take him back with me."

"And then?"

"The usual business."

They were silent for a while. Then she said: "I wonder what sort of a person he is?"

"They are all much of a muchness."

"Are they?"

"Yes."

"What exactly does that mean?"

"They are always pretty cheapjack people. The ones who do it without any real motive. You can't often have much pity for them."

"You believe that?"

He lifted his shoulders.

"That's all I could believe," he said. "I couldn't do my job if I allowed myself to believe anything else."

"And yet," she said thoughtfully, "they must all be different, mustn't they? If you could ever get really inside their hearts, their minds, they must all be different."

He did not answer. He knew that this was the kind of talk that he always had to school himself against. This was the very first lesson, and the one he had always found it hardest to learn.

"Suppose, for example," she went on, "that you arrested a man and he turned out to be—simple?"

"Simple?"

"Imbecile."

"That's just what this one most probably is," he said.

"You think so?"

Did she jump then? he asked himself suddenly. Did she clutch at something with her mind when I said that? Did she? He felt himself tingling a bit as he watched her more closely. He waited to see if she said something more, but she was waiting for him to answer.

"I think he most probably is," he said at last.

"What would happen in a case like that?" she asked.

He thought he had imagined things again. Her voice was still as soft and unruffled as ever.

"How do you mean, what happens?"

"Well, what do you do in a case like that?"

"I don't do anything. That's not my job. That's for the court to decide."

"And if the court thinks that someone is like that?"

"Well then, they deal with it accordingly."

"Do they always find out?"

"Yes."

"Do you really think they do? One hears such confused stories. Do you really think they find out the truth about that sort of thing?"

"Yes. It's very, very unlikely that they ever make a mistake about that."

"And they don't . . ." she stopped in the middle of her sentence.

"They don't what?"

"They don't hang anyone if he really didn't know what he was doing?"

"If he is genuinely insane, of course they don't."

"Do they put him somewhere where they take care of him?"

"Something like that. It's a bit off my beat really."

"Of course." She spoke as if chiding herself for asking foolish questions. And then she fell silent as if she were thinking deeply. He sat and watched her, wondering. He felt sure that something was coming from her, although he did not know what and he did not know when. And he was equally sure that it would only come if he waited for it, and that if he dug for it, if he pressed her at all, if he even coaxed her, then it would not come at all. The only fact he had was the knowledge that someone had been to the house that night and that she had lied about it. Beyond that he had nothing. He could not say with logical certainty that the person who had been to the house was the man he was after. Yet he felt quite sure it was. Did she know where he had gone to now? Did she know where he was hiding? He could not properly answer those questions for himself yet. He only knew that she had something to tell him, and vaguely he sensed that there was something she wanted to tell him. And he told himself again, carefully and deliberately, that he must wait for it to come and not try to pull it out of her. She is obstructing you, he told himself. She is holding you up on the search, and that puts you against each other. By all the rules you and she are dead against each other. But that isn't the way it's going to come from her. She isn't going to give it like that. If you show that you are against her, she is going to shut down like a watertight door. It's this other thing that's going to bring it from her. It's this other thing you felt the moment you came into the room, the moment you saw her at the door even. You bristled the moment Bond said his first rough word to her, and she knew that, and now even if you tried you can't feel against her, and she knows that too. You've got to wait and let it come her own way, if you want it at all. Are you sure she isn't just delaying you? Just holding you back from the search? Yes, you're sure, you fool, you know you're sure. You can't pin things like that down to reason, but you just know it.

He stood there, feeling the warmth of the fire creeping into him, and again there was a silence that had no awkwardness in it and that did not clamour for any sudden breaking.

Presently she said:

"I never asked you what your name was, did I?"

"Wilson," he said. "And I never asked you what yours was?"

"Maldon," she told him. And then, "Do you come from London, Mr. Wilson?" And she asked it him in a deliberately formal manner, as if the fact of their being strangers was merely a pretence, so that the careful use of the prefix to his name was almost a jest between them.

"I do," he said.

"Have you always lived there?"

"Most of the time, on and off."

"I suppose you feel more at home there than you do out in the wilds."

"I suppose I do."

"You don't sound over certain of that."

He laughed.

"I think I hate London really," he said.

"Why? What do you find wrong with it?"

"In my job I only see the rotten side of it, perhaps that's why."

She thought for a moment, and then said:

"But there's a rotten side to so many things. You must never condemn the whole thing because you are only thinking of the rotten side of it. Wherever you go there is a good side and a bad side. It's so often a matter of point of view, isn't it?"

"Perhaps. But if you are forced to look at something from the same point of view for long enough, you are apt to become unconscious of any other point of view."

Now he wanted to tell her of the things he hated and the things that were nagging at his mind so often, the things that had been piling up inside him for so long. He knew that if ever he poured it all out he would like it to be to her, and suddenly, as he stood there looking at her, fiercely and passionately he wanted the power to tear away the blindness from her, so that he could talk to her with nothing to hold him back. And then as quickly he kicked the thought aside because he knew in his heart that her blindness was nothing, it made no shield, no barrier between them. He wanted, suddenly deep inside him, to know her and to see her and to talk to her as an ordinary person in an ordinary way, without any suspicions, without any things to find out from her, without any thoughts of his job or of anything else or of anyone else. And suddenly, slapping into him, jolting him, she spoke as if she knew what his thought had been.

"Did you ever know anyone who was blind before?"

"No, I don't think I did."

She waited for a moment, and then said quietly: "I thought you had."

"Why? What made you think that?"

She waited now for several seconds before she said: "It's just the way you've talked."

"What way have I talked?"

"It's just that I haven't heard pity lurking at the back of your voice. It's funny what a lot that can mean."

"But surely, people . . ." His words petered out because he did not know quite what he was going to say.

She laughed very quietly, thoughtfully.

"They mean well," she said. "Of course they mean well." And then her voice became quicker and brisker as she said: "Sorry! Sorry, but I just felt I wanted to say it. What's the time?"

He looked at his watch.

"It's just after eleven," he said. He was wondering how much longer he could stay there.

"Surely it's no earthly good your going out and looking tonight, is it?" she asked him.

"I don't know."

"You'll simply wander about in the snow, getting colder and colder . . ." she broke off, then added: "You'll have to sleep somewhere, sometime, won't you?"

"Yes," he answered, doubtfully.

She stood up from her chair.

"I think I shall go to bed now," she said. "But if you like you are very welcome to try and get a bit of sleep here in front of the fire, so you can start off again as soon as it's daylight."

She made the offer casually, as if it did not matter to her either way. But when he did not answer, after she had waited for him to speak, she said: "I should do that if I were you. It's much more sensible, isn't it?" And now her voice was soft and persuasive.

He was thinking about the night outside, the darkness and the thick snow and the cold and the wet of it all, and the hopelessness of looking in that storm, and he was thinking too that he wanted to cling somehow to this house, to keep in touch with her because he still felt, stronger than ever, that something was coming from her soon. It was easy to make up his mind.

"If you wouldn't think it an awful nuisance of me, I'd like to do that very much."

She turned and walked across the room towards the door.

"Keep the fire going so that you don't get cold," she said, "and I'll bring you down a couple of blankets in a minute."

"Please don't trouble to do that."

"It isn't any trouble," she laughed. "Why do you keep thinking everything is a trouble? If you must know I am quite glad to have some company in the house tonight."

He heard her going up the stairs, and moving in one of the rooms above, and then she was coming down again. She came back into the room with blankets over her arm.

"Here you are," she said. "Make yourself as cosy as you can. I should take your shoes and socks off if I were you, in case they are wet."

He went over and took the blankets from her arm. "Thank you," he said.

She turned to go, but paused in the doorway and said: "Unless Bond comes back, that is."

"Yes, of course," he said. "I understand."

He stood in front of the fire watching her go from the room again and hearing her walk up the stairs. He stood there for quite a long time, until the padding of her feet on the floor above stopped, and he heard the faint creaking of her bed.

Then he took off his jacket and his shoes and wrapped the blankets around him, and settled down in the armchair before the fire. He left the door of the room a few inches open. He had no intention of going to sleep and he wanted to be able to hear the slightest sound throughout the house. He lit a cigarette and drank a little of the whisky from the flask in his pocket. The dampness of his outside clothes had left him shivery, even in front of the fire.

The house was very quiet now. He sat there, looking into the fire, trying to clear his thoughts. But his mind was confused and it would not clear itself.

The chase, the search for the murderer; Bond and his gun, the snow and the girl upstairs; they were all mixed up together and with other things. He was worried and vaguely unhappy. It was not because of new things that he was worried. He was worried more because of some of the things that had been in his mind so much before, so often and so naggingly.

He was thinking about his last few years and the more he thought about them the more he hated them. He could see himself back in a thousand situations, hating himself in them all. There was never anything clear and clean, never any gift without a hook in it, never any meeting without some undercover deceit. He knew it was this girl who had brought it all on again. But it wasn't new, it had nagged at him for ages. It was just that she had brought the feeling back to him more strongly. He thought of himself, not so many years back, entering the police college. You thought it was going to be exciting then, he reminded himself. You thought it was going to be a romantic life. The detective of the story books. The brilliant deductions and the battles of wits, a fascinating game. You didn't know you were simply putting your head into a world that stinks from top to bottom. You didn't know you were choosing the life of a garbage man, digging and prodding and letting the smell out from human dregs. Where and when have you had your battles of wits? All you've done and all you're likely to do, nine-tenths of the time, is to look for evidence and all of the boredom and the filthy, sneaking, peeping that the word means.

This job out here is a breath of fresh air compared with the things you usually have to do. Evidence, get evidence, get evidence. They usually knew who'd done the job, and all they had to do was to find ways of pinning it. That's your man. Watch him until he trips. Watch him, follow him, get near him, smell him, trail him, track him, trip him if you can. Get round his friends. Perhaps his wife will give him away. Get evidence, get evidence. The stinking drabness of it all made his mind revolt as he thought of it. How many hours have you stood in back street doorways, knowing who'd done it, waiting for the proof? How many hundreds and thousands of hours? No, by golly, James, don't add them up, you can't bear it. Forget them, forget they ever happened. Pretend each time is the first time, that's your only chance. And when did you last meet someone fair and square? When did you last meet anyone so that you and he, or you and she, were able to take each other as you found each other? It's always part of this evidence, evidence, evidence. It'll pay you to have a talk with so-and-so. You may pick up a line there. That girl at Jack's Club used to know him, have a talk with her. Everyone you ever meet. And it's the same with them, the other way round, in that under layer of London that your nose is always poked into. 'He's a cop. I seem to know his face. Watch your mouth.' You can hear it even when it isn't said. It grows on you. It eats right into you. You're never off your guard, never off the job. And that first lesson. Never soften up. No sentiment. That first lesson, that hopelessly hard first lesson. It took you some learning, he thought, even if you've learnt it now. I don't believe you have. Although it's not for want of trying. You tried pretty hard in self-defence, after you had tripped pretty hard once or twice in your green days. That little hat-check girl in the club that covered the gambling place behind Shaftesbury Avenue. Myra. You cleaned that job pretty well, and you got a pat on the back for it, too, and Myra didn't know about what happened behind the doors. Myra was crying that night because she thought that somehow she had got mixed up with things she didn't know about. She didn't want her mother to know, and when she cried her eyes seemed to get bigger and bluer, and her mouth went softer, trembly, and you were a knight in armour riding in and rescuing her from the wicked people who had tricked her. By golly, yes, you were a knight all right, but without the armour. Your heart gave a jump and your legs felt flabby, and you wanted to pick her up in your arms and carry her away somewhere so that she'd be safe forever afterwards. And you practically did that, too. You were shy about it, weren't you? Shy to let any of the fellows know, because you knew they would laugh sarcastically, and say they had heard it all before, and you knew they were wrong. You knew that in this case it really was the sweet little girl who nearly came unstuck. It was funny how shy you were about it. When you took her to the races that day you could hardly look at her, or look at the races, or look at anything, because you were so anxiously watching to make sure none of the fellows were there to laugh at you. But you knew they'd be wrong if they laughed this time. This was really something. Something rather beautiful. Something that got inside you, too. You carried that photo of her for a long, long time, and sometimes then those days you felt that photo in your pocket, and the pavements you spent such a lot of your time on seemed springy and good to walk on. And you were counting your savings and trying to reckon when you'd get more, and your mind was full of dreamy things. Until that night when you tore the photograph up into little tiny pieces, and chucked your beer over them, and wondered if you would ever have the face to walk into the station again next morning. That was the night you heard she had been taken in under her real name, with a record worth a couple of columns in the popular press. That was part of your first lesson all right, and that did something to you. After that, you'd have looked at your own kid sister with suspicion in your mind. It killed something in you. Especially for women. And it was killed still worse when you knew you could have a dozen every night, just by crooking your finger, with nothing to pay, just in exchange for shutting your eyes to something. In the café, the late one on the corner, they would laugh in his face and offer themselves, "Do you want to sleep with me, Mr. Wilson?" It was only a joke with them, because they knew what the answer would be. But they would have liked it if it could have been not a joke; not because of the sleeping, but because of the tags it would have given them on him afterwards. Knowing that, it made you hate them, and it gradually made you think they were all the same. You knew they weren't, really, you knew it was nonsense, but gradually it came eating into you, and you couldn't meet anyone fair and square somehow.

His mind went roving around, back away behind him, and the places and the things and the people started streaming past, and he thought of all the places and the people like Peter and Smudge Anderson, and Johnson the late lamented Johnson and Smooth Harry and the girl with the very black hair who had her throat cut and Tommy the Tapper. Yes, old Tommy the Tapper, he would still be doing it now. Tommy the Tapper, with his white-painted stick, and the placard across his chest to say he was blind. The tap tap tap of Tommy's stick on the pavements had helped many a pretty little party to break up before the police arrived. "Only a poor blind man, sir, feeling my way along." Tap tap tap, the stick had a lump of metal on the end, and it echoed on the pavements, and old Tommy never let them down. He was one of the most reliable lookouts in town, and he was just about as blind as a man in an observatory. But he took some tripping, Tommy did. There were none so blind as the ones who got well paid to be. The towns were full of phoney blinds, and it usually paid pretty well, one way or another. All right, all right, James Wilson nagged himself, you don't particularly want to think of Tommy the Tapper now. What makes you think of him now? What makes you, at this particular moment and in this particular place, start thinking about the phoney blinds? In heaven's name, what? Couldn't that be the one thing you didn't have to think of, just now? Couldn't you just keep your mind off Tommy the Tapper? Anything else, but just not that. Not now, not while you are in this house. Anything else except Tommy the Tapper and the phoney blinds.

He sat there in front of the fire, bitterly hating and despising the life he led, the job he had chosen to do. He had thought about it often before, but now it was coming at him stronger and deeper. He was hating himself at the moment because of the girl who was sleeping upstairs. He knew she had lied to him, but he had kept it from her that he knew. He had talked to her, sat with her, shared something with her somehow, and all the while pretending that he did not suspect her at all. He wanted to meet her clean and fair, and already it was dirtied. But she was deceiving you, that makes you quits, he argued to himself. No, it doesn't, you know it really doesn't. She's got some reason, some real reason, something that matters deep inside her. With you it's nothing that matters inside you, it's the dirty paraphernalia of what you're always doing. You were sharing something with her, something that you couldn't quite understand, but it was there and yet you've had to soil it all the time.

He pulled out his packet of cigarettes, and took one out and lighted it, and dragged at it hard, just two or three times, and then snatched it from his mouth and leaned over and squashed it out against the brick of the fireplace. And he watched it as the paper split and the charred tobacco spewed out, and then the brown tobacco from farther up, and he watched it closely, concentrating on it, focusing his thoughts on it. Look, it started to telescope itself with the pressure, and the pressure was a bit too much and it bent itself over and then the paper split. And you had only taken two or three puffs out of it, too. You've certainly spoiled it now, you couldn't light it again now if you tried, it has split down the side and it wouldn't draw anymore. What a whoop of joy that one would bring from a man who picks ends up from the pavement. Just two or three puffs, and now you've crushed it to bits, and you seem to forget that cigarettes cost money, and they are meant to be smoked all the way through instead of being crushed out after a couple of puffs. Look how the paper bends and gives, and then suddenly splits in a straight line up the side. Isn't that interesting. Isn't that damned interesting. It was a famous painting, not a sculpture or a film star but a famous painting, that's what it was. The paper suddenly splits and then the tobacco comes spewing out. Yes, it was a famous painting that you saw reproduced in a magazine somewhere. He was trying real hard to force his mind on to the simple material things in front of his eyes, but it wasn't any good and he had to give up trying and he had to think of the things that were whirling round inside him.

He lay there in the chair with the blankets round him, twisting and turning restlessly. And suddenly he was stiff and tense, his spine tingling, holding his breath and listening. There was a step in the passage outside the room, a slow, soft step. He thought he must have been asleep. He heard the step coming towards the door, and with a quick movement he threw the blankets aside and slipped swiftly across to the wall beside the fireplace so that his figure should not be outlined by the dim glow of the fire. He pressed himself against the wall, taut and ready, waiting for the door to open.

The footsteps stopped. There was silence for a moment, but the door was not pushed open. Instead he heard a gentle tapping on it. He waited, then the tapping came a little louder. His hands and his body were ready, but his voice was tight.

"Who's that?"

His heart was pumping with sudden relief as he heard her voice.

"May I come in?"

"Yes, of course."

She pushed the door open slowly and walked into the room.

"Did I wake you? Did I startle you?"

"No," he said.

He was slightly bewildered and he knew that he must have been to sleep. He moved away from the wall, back in front of the fire, and quickly collected the blankets from the floor, so that they would not be in her way. She came slowly across the room. She was wearing a long green dressing-gown that came right down to her feet.

"Do you mind if I come and talk to you?" she said.

"Sit down in the chair there," he answered. "I'll poke the fire up a bit."

He started to fiddle the logs about, coaxing them into a little crackle of flame. He waited for her to speak again.

"Have you been to sleep?" she asked.

"I think I must have been. Haven't you?"

She shook her head.

"No. I've been trying to think."

He waited again. He knew that something was coming from her now, and he did not want to prompt it or coax it in case he drove it back again. She was sitting in her chair, the chair in which he had been sprawling before. He pulled up another chair in front of the fire and sat down.

They waited in silence for quite a long time. Stronger than ever now he had the feeling that they were sharing something, that they were not against each other, but were together; and the silence rested easily between them, like a comfortable sympathy. When at last she spoke it was an unexpected question.

"What is your first name?" she asked.

"James," he said.

"James." She repeated it softly, slowly, thoughtfully. Then she waited again, but he knew that she was not waiting for him to speak, but waiting for her own thoughts to form themselves into words.

"A first name sometimes makes a person seem so different," she said slowly.

"In what way?"

"Not always," she said, "but sometimes. Not just by knowing it and not just by speaking it, but if you think of someone by their first name, if you really think of them that way, then it makes a lot of difference sometimes."

She was silent again, and again he waited for her.

"Do you know what I mean?" she asked him.

He could not honestly answer that he did.

"Partly, not quite," he said.

"I mean that when you think of people by their surnames, or when you think of them without any names at all, then they are impersonal beings, they are remote creatures, nothing very much to do with you, not touching you intimately. They are meaningless, silhouettes on a screen, without any human warmth or meaning for you, and sometimes when you think of them by their first names, when you actually *think* of them that way, it makes them different."

"Mmm . . ."

He made a noncommittal sound just to help her along. "I don't think I am explaining what I mean very well," she said. "Perhaps it isn't a real thing after all. I just had a feeling that it was."

She stopped talking again, and the silence in the room seemed deeper than before, an extra hush had fallen across them. And he knew that both their minds and both their hearts were somehow stilled, waiting together, waiting for something that mattered in the same way or in different ways to both of them. When she spoke again her voice was a whisper, as if to herself or to no one, or as if it were a prayer.

"My brother's name is Danny," she said.

FIVE

In the stillness of the room, the old instinctive things came prodding at James Wilson. This was the moment to jump at her, question after question, quickly, breaking her pre-arranged thoughts, tripping her, frightening her, making it all come quickly. Where was he now? Where did he go? What time did he come here? How long did he wait here? What did he say? What is he wearing? The old quick pestering routine. They prodded at James Wilson now instinctively, but they made no impact on him. They belonged to the world of being against someone. They had no place among things that were being shared. He waited patiently. He waited for when she wanted to speak again. He knew it was coming, and he knew what it was meaning to her. He wanted to touch her, gently, comfortingly, but he sat where he was and left her with her thoughts. There was no pretence at hiding things now. Whether he had suspected or not was a trifling thing that did not matter to her now.

Her voice was level and perfectly composed when she spoke again.

"Bond means to kill Danny. I could feel it in him."

The worries that James Wilson had felt about Bond came vividly at him again now. He was suddenly fearful that even at this moment Bond might be doing anything. He wanted to reassure her, to tell her that his job was to stop that, and that he was going to do his job, but the thought of Bond out there now, out of his control, made the words strangle in his throat.

"I cannot bring myself to blame Bond," she said. "If his daughter has . . . suffered, I cannot bring myself to blame him for anything. Don't think I am hard and inhuman talking about it coldly like this. When you have lived with a fear of something at the back of your mind for long enough, when you have known in your heart for a long time that something might happen in the end, then when it comes you find yourself dealing with it differently, that's all."

"Yes," he said. The picture that her words unfolded was vague and indefinite, yet vividly real and complete at the same time.

She said: "I had to come and talk to you now because there is a chance, and because somehow I feel it is the only chance."

"Yes." He was merely groping his way with her and speaking only to help her along.

"Bond has gone somewhere now," she said. "He won't find Danny, I'm sure of that. But while Bond is away you could go and fetch Danny. And once you had Danny in your charge, then Bond couldn't kill him, could he?"

"No."

"You could fetch him, before Bond comes back."

"Where is he, then?"

She did not seem to hear his question. She was too deep in what she was saying and what she was trying to say.

"Danny isn't . . . Danny doesn't always know what he is doing."

She lowered her head, and passed a hand wearily across her forehead and in front of her eyes.

"I've tried so hard to look after him, to keep him out of trouble. And now I seem to have failed him."

James Wilson wished he could say something, wished he could help to make the telling of it easier for her.

She said: "He came here this evening. He had been away for three days, and I was afraid something terrible might have happened. He came and he was gone again quite a long while before you arrived. You must have been a long way behind him."

"Yes. We had lost a lot of time. We had really lost track of him altogether."

"You only came here by chance, then?"

"Yes. We saw the house, and we had to look somewhere. At first we were trying to make for that light that I told you we saw. But we couldn't seem to trace it."

"The light, yes." She paused, as if thinking about it. Then she went on: "Most of the heavy snow fell between the time he went and the time you came. It was coming down so heavily then that I thought it might well have covered up his footmarks. But I couldn't be sure, of course. When you went out and looked, with the lantern, I could only sit and hope. But if you did not see anything, it isn't likely that Bond did, is it?"

"No. The snow had covered everything. I'm sure of that."

She seemed to relax a little, as if comforted by what he said.

"I only hope you are right," she said. "I pray that Bond does not find him."

Her thoughts were outside of the room now, outside hiding

desperately somewhere in the snow. James Wilson did not hurry her. She was telling it now, and he waited for her to go on.

"He came here and he told me what had happened. He told me everything. At least"—she made a little gesture with her hand—"I suppose he told me everything. He usually tells me everything." She half-turned her face towards him, and spoke as if asking for his confirmation. "He told me about two children."

James Wilson knew it was not being easy for her to keep her voice so steady and controlled.

"Yes," he said quietly. "There were two. The first one was killed. The second one was Bond's. She isn't dead."

"Danny's always been like that with me. He has always told me everything." She raised her shoulders slowly, then dropped them again. "Not that it makes much difference now," she said.

She touched her eyes with the back of her fingers one after the other. He thought she was stopping a tear from coming. But her voice was still toneless and unwavering.

"When he came here, he was puffed from running hard. He told me that he had stolen a car, and that it had skidded and he had to leave it where it was. He had been running all the rest of the way. He was very frightened."

She shook her head slowly, as if the remembering of it made her feel bewildered.

"I didn't know what to do. I asked him if he was being followed, and he said yes, and then he said no, and then yes again, and no again. By that time he did not know what he was saying. I wanted to wait, I wanted to calm him down so that he would be able to tell me about it more clearly. I wanted to tell him what was best for him to do. I wanted to do everything I could to help him." She turned her head towards James Wilson again. "He's my brother," she said.

"Yes." He spoke softly.

"But he was very frightened. And for almost the first time in his life, he wouldn't listen to me at all. He has always listened to me. Always. But tonight he kept talking all the time, and I could hardly get a word in. It was because he was so frightened. He kept talking all the time, quickly. Some of the time I could hardly understand what he was saying."

She leaned forward in her chair, resting her head in her hands. The room was so quiet that it stretched out the time and made it seem like several minutes before she spoke again.

"You might never have found him. Even now, you might never find him." She shrugged her shoulders again, slowly, wearily. "But I don't know. I suppose you would, in the end. Somebody would, sooner or later. And anything is better than to have him found by . . . someone like Bond."

She turned suddenly towards him, full face, as if she were seeing him.

"He needs to be taken care of," she said eagerly and pleadingly. "Danny isn't like other people. He needs to be taken care of. It ought to have happened ages ago. I ought never to have tried to look after him. But somehow it seemed kinder." She hesitated. "He is perfectly all right some of the time," she added.

Now her fingers were tapping on the arm of the chair, as if she were trying to steady herself.

"Will you promise me?" she asked suddenly.

"Promise you what?"

"I didn't have to tell you all this. I don't have to tell you where he is now. You might never find him. I don't have to tell you. You can't make me. I'm only doing it because . . . because of Bond. I'm terrified of Bond finding him. That's why I'm telling you, so that you can fetch him before Bond finds him. You won't hurt him. I know you won't hurt him. You'll see that they take care of him, won't you? Put him somewhere to be taken care of, properly, kindly. You will, won't you? Promise me."

"I'll . . . I won't hurt him, no."

"But promise me he won't be punished for something he didn't know he was doing. Promise me."

"I . . ." he hesitated, fumbling for his words. He did not want to be glib with her.

"Why won't you say? Why are you hesitating?"

"It's because . . . I have no control about those things. I don't decide. It's not in my hands."

She sat there, silently. He waited for her to speak again, but she said nothing. He shifted uneasily in his chair. He did not want to say things to her just for smoothness.

"I can't actually promise things that are not in my power," he said at last. "But if he is . . . like that . . . then he will be properly taken care of. He will be sent somewhere. I am sure of that. You can be sure of that, too."

She nodded her head slowly.

"If you say that, yes. If you say that, I believe it." As she spoke, he was feeling strangely glad that he had only said the things he could truly say.

Now he asked her, gently, "Where has he gone to?"

"He has gone to his hut."

James Wilson's mind went flashing back to the barns along the lane. But she soon pulled him back.

"His hut up on the hill," she said. "His own beloved hut." Her last words were more to herself than to him.

"On the hill?"

"Yes. There is a hill right opposite the house here. Quite a high one. That light you said you saw, that must have been him."

"But you said there was no . . ." he broke off his words as he realised what a fool he was being.

She said, very evenly and steadily: "He is my brother. For as long as I thought it was best for him, I had prepared myself to tell every lie I could think of."

He did not answer her. He could think of nothing.

She went on: "Up on the hill there, is a little hut. It is really a shepherd's hut. It is high up the hill, and it not much used now, because they have not had sheep grazing on the hill there for a long time. But Danny often goes there. He likes it up there. He went up there tonight. He took some food with him, and said he was going to hide there for a while."

"He got up there before the really heavy snow?"

"He went up during the storm. It must have taken him quite a time to get up. It is a long way. And it would be very difficult in the snow. But of course he knows the path well."

"Could I find the path?"

"Not while it is dark. But as soon as it is light, I think you could. The snow would hide the path, of course, but you could find it by the contour of the ground if I explained it. That was what I was thinking. If you went directly it was light in the morning, you could fetch him before Bond had a chance to find him."

"If Bond doesn't come back first."

"I am praying that he does not," she said simply.

"I will go the moment it is light. How do I find the path?"

"I think I can explain it to you so that you cannot miss it. I can remember it well. I knew it before I had the trouble with my eyes." As she said that, he looked at her with a crowd of new thoughts tumbling into his mind. But she gave him no time for them.

"The path itself is not likely to be thickly snowed up," she said. "I asked Danny, before he went up tonight, whether it wouldn't be getting impassable in the snow. He said that he had been up it before, through the heaviest snow, and that it never piled thick on the path because of the curious formation of the ground." She made a movement with her hand, as if trying to describe it visually to him. "It is like a long knife-edge of ground, sloping steeply upwards. The ground falls away sharply on both sides of it. The knife-edge curves right the way up, almost to the spot where the hut is. The snow might drift and bank on one side or the other, but on the crest, where the path is, it is too narrow and exposed for the snow to pile. It's probably slippery, though," she added quickly.

"Where does it start?"

"There are two barns, close together, down the lane between here and the road. It starts almost exactly opposite them. In the daylight you cannot fail to notice that high, sharp edge. Even the snow won't hide the shape of it."

"How high up is the hut?"

"Half a mile? More than that, I should think. When you get to the top of that path, the ground flattens for a bit, and then you can see the hut."

"Is the hut not visible from here?"

"No, because it lies back a little on the flat part of the hill."

Her voice for the last few minutes now had been limp and dull and lifeless. It was as if she suddenly felt herself to be at the mercy of something that was outside her control. She had told him everything now. She had dropped her guard completely. It felt to James Wilson as if someone had placed in his hands a trust. It had come so freely, without his prodding, without his even asking. He looked at her and knew that he was glad.

"I'll find it," he said. "I'll go as soon as it is light."

"Yes." She hesitated a moment. "You'll . . .?" her voice was awkward, and she did not finish speaking the question. He waited, but still she did not finish it.

"What were you going to ask?"

She shook her head.

"No," she said. "There isn't any need. I think you understand. I know you do."

"Yes," he said. He wished he could think of something to say to her. She shivered slightly.

"Wrap the blankets round you," she said. "You must be cold."

"I'm all right."

"It must be about three in the morning, mustn't it?"

He looked at his watch.

"It's after that. Nearly half-past."

"There's no use your trying to find the path till it is light. You might as well get some sleep. I will wake you again near the time."

"I'm not sleepy. I don't think I shall sleep."

"You might as well try. I'll come down and wake you."

"Are you going up again now, then?"

"Yes. I suppose so." It sounded as if nothing mattered. He wanted her to stay. He could not tell whether it would be easier for her to be alone or to have someone with her. But apart from that, he wanted her to stay.

"I'm not sleepy," he said again.

"Shall I get you a hot drink? Would you like some more cocoa?"

"No, really, thank you."

"It will be cold up on the hill tonight," she said softly.

He did not answer. She still stayed, sitting in the chair, leaning over towards the fire, making no move to go upstairs. Presently she said:

"I wish I could think things out more clearly. I wish everything didn't have to be so muddled. If it had not been for Bond, I don't know whether or not I would have told you. I just don't know. It is all so muddled. I didn't know what was right or what was best."

"You've done what's best for him," James Wilson said. He wanted to ease things for her, but he knew it sounded empty.

She suddenly stiffened in her chair.

"What was that?" she whispered.

Her head was up and her lips were apart as she listened intently. He had not heard anything. As they sat there, listening, the silence of the night seemed like a solid hovering thing.

Then he heard it, heard something. It sounded like the clicking of the latch on the outside door. The single tiny sound sent a hollow echo through the silence of the house. James Wilson was stiff and tense in his chair now. His head was half-turned towards the door of the room. He flicked his eyes over to look at the girl. She was facing round towards the door. They heard the sound again, unmistakable now. And then there were steps in the passage outside. They were slow, tiptoe, concealed, unrecognisable steps, coming towards the room. The girl stood up from her chair and took a couple of steps towards the door. She was facing directly at the door of the room, one hand held slightly out towards it. James Wilson could see that she was ready to speak to him the moment he came into the room, before he could say anything or do anything. They waited. The steps came on, and paused outside the door of the room. Then the door was flung suddenly open.

James Wilson saw the burly figure there just in time. The girl's hand was going out towards him in a welcoming, pleading gesture. She was going to speak to him. James Wilson could see that she was just about to speak to him. He put out his own hand, in a futile attempt to warn her, to stop her. He wanted to shout to her to stop her from speaking, to stop her from using the name she was just going to use. For a horrible, strangled moment his mind would not click into place. All he could think of was that she was going to say it and he'd got to stop her, got to stop her. It was only a second or so, but to him it seemed to stretch out into minutes, like a dumb charade, while his tongue seemed to swell in the back of his throat and his mind wouldn't work. And then, just in time, before she could speak, he turned to the doorway and blurted out: "Bond!"

He heard the sudden drawing in of her breath, saw her outstretched arm stiffen for a moment and then drop slowly to her side. She was swaying very slightly. He thought she was going to faint. He stepped quickly over to her, and took hold of her arm with his hand, and gently but firmly turned her round and led her back to her chair.

Bond stood in the open doorway without saying a word, glaring at each of them in turn. His shotgun was in his hands, pointing into the room. He looked very carefully and deliberately round the room, as if he half-expected to find someone else there. James Wilson had moved away from the girl again now, and was standing in front of the fire. He was staring at Bond dully, as if his presence hardly seemed to make sense.

Bond walked forward into the middle of the room. He stood right in front of James Wilson, and then raised his gun slowly and deliberately. Almost on a level with James Wilson's eyes, he broke the gun open and eased the two cartridges slightly out. Then he looked challengingly into James Wilson's eyes, and pushed the cartridges home again and snapped the gun shut. He lowered the gun into the crook of his arm, and stood waiting for one of them to speak. He waited in silence. Neither of them said anything. At last he spoke to James Wilson.

"What's the idea?"

"Idea of what?"

"Taking the cartridges out of my gun. You did it."

James Wilson did not answer.

"You did it!" Bond said again. "You must have done it. Nobody else could have done it."

"I took them out, yes." The answer was cold and calm.

"What for?"

"Because you were too keen on pointing it at anyone and everyone. I thought it might go off."

Bond brought his head forward in a threatening kind of way.

"You think you're going to save him, don't you? Well, you're not. Nobody's going to save him. I'm going to find him and nothing is going to save him."

His voice had gone into a growling croak again. James Wilson wanted to look at the girl, to see if she was showing anything. But he dared not look at her too obviously, in case it showed his thoughts to Bond.

But Bond was looking at her now, gazing at her as if he had suddenly seen her for the first time.

"What are you two doing together?" he demanded. "What have you been talking about?" He swung round on James Wilson. "You've not been looking for him. Why haven't you been looking for him?" He stopped, and then lowered his voice almost to a whisper. "I believe you know where he is," he said slowly.

"Don't talk like a fool, Bond!" James Wilson snapped it out quickly, to cover up in case the girl should make any sound to give herself away.

"What have you been talking about together? Why have you been waiting here so long?"

"I've been waiting here because it is impossible to do any more searching on a night like this.”

“Haven’t you been outside the house at all since I left you?”

“Yes. I had a look round. But I gave it up.” He wished he was not answering the questions. He wished he could shake off this business of letting himself be cross-examined by Bond.

“Did you make those footprints leading down to the barns, down the lane?”

“Yes. Those are mine.”

“Was one of the barns locked when you went there?”

“Yes.”

“You didn’t look inside that one, then?”

“No.”

“How do you know there’s nobody in that one?”

“Because it’s padlocked on the outside. Nobody could have hidden in there and then fixed the padlock on the outside of the door.”

“But, somebody else could.” Bond leaned towards him, looking at him meaningly. “Somebody else could have locked that door, on the outside, to make it look good.”

Bond turned, very slowly and deliberately, towards the girl.

“She might have done it, for instance.”

“She didn’t. Don’t be a fool!”

“How do you know she didn’t? You’re on her side. You’re trying to cover her up all the time. There’s something funny here, and you’re trying to cover it up.”

James Wilson did not answer him. His hands were beginning to tighten with fury, but inside his stomach there was a hollow feeling.

“How do you know she didn’t lock that door?” Bond asked again.

“Because she hasn’t been outside the house all the evening.” It was difficult to stop answering the questions with the hollow feeling in his stomach.

“Just because she says so? You take it for granted that she’s speaking the truth. I tell you she’s hiding something. You’re both hiding something!”

He swung round on the girl again.

“When did you last go down to that barn?”

“I—I can’t remember. Several days ago. I don’t often go there.”

“What’s in the barn?”

“Machines. Farming machines.”

“Did you go there tonight?”

"I just told you. I haven't been there for days."

"I asked you if you'd been down there tonight. Have you?"

James Wilson was listening, and having to grip hard hold of himself. He wanted to shut Bond up, and just at that moment he could have hit him again and loved it. But he pressed his lips together and tried to hold himself. He knew if he tried to stop Bond's questions, he would only be adding to his suspicions.

The girl did not answer the last question. She appeared to ignore it deliberately. James Wilson could see that it would take more than Bond to ruffle her outward composure.

"I believe you know where he is," Bond said again. "I believe you both know. There's something funny about this place. There's something funny about the way you've suddenly stopped searching. There's something funny about the two of you talking together in the middle of the night like this."

The hollow feeling inside James Wilson would not go away.

"Where's the key to that barn?" Bond threw the question out so abruptly that the sudden sound made the girl start.

"The key? I think it is kept in the house here."

"You think? Do you mean you're not sure where it is?"

"It's kept in the house here."

"Where is it?"

"It's hanging in the hall, just inside the front door."

Bond stood for a moment, undecided. Then he turned and went out of the room into the passage. He was not soft-footed any longer. He was clumping his way around noisily.

He called back into the room from the passage. "There's a whole row of keys here. Which one is it?"

She turned her head towards the door and answered him.

"I don't know which nail it is on. But each key has a piece of wood tied to it with string. It's the second largest piece of wood."

They could hear Bond's voice muttering: "A damn silly way to identify keys." And James Wilson's nails were digging into the flesh in the palms of his hands.

Bond came back into the room, swinging one of the keys on its string. For the first time, James Wilson noticed how tired the man looked. He had been on the go solidly, both with his body and his nerves, and now he was beginning to look dragged out with fatigue.

He stood there holding the gun in one hand and dangling the key in the other.

"Are you coming down to look in that barn with me, Wilson?"

"No, I'm damned if I am. There's no one in there."

"You've stopped looking. You're not making any attempt to search for him now. Why? What are you up to?"

"I'm simply waiting till there's a chance to go on looking. It's no good tonight."

"You can look in that barn just as well now as any time."

"I tell you there's no one in the barn."

"Just because she says so. That's not enough for me. All right, I'll go alone."

He clumped out of the room, and they heard him go across the passage and out through the front door. They heard the front door slam behind him.

For a minute or two they waited there in silence. Each knew what the other was thinking, but they hesitated to put the thoughts into words.

She was the first to speak. Her voice was hushed and colourless.

"What are you going to do now?"

"I don't know. I'm trying to think."

She stood up from her chair.

"I think I'll . . . go up." Her voice was wobbling a little.

He laid a hand lightly on her arm.

"Please, if you can, stay down here till Bond comes back."

"Why?"

"You can go up as soon as he is back. But it would be much better not to go before then."

"Why?"

"Because of the state he is in. He'll pick on anything. If you're not in the room here when he comes in again, that will be quite enough to set him off. He'll think you have sneaked away somewhere. He'll come barging upstairs looking for you."

She shrugged her shoulders slowly.

"What does it matter? What does it matter now? You'll never be able to get up to the hut without him going with you. He knows. He knows there's something."

"No. He can't know. How can he?"

"But he obviously does. He obviously suspects."

"He suspects, yes. But he doesn't know. He can't know."

"What makes him suspect? What makes him keep saying that you know where Danny is?"

"He's under a strain. He's half mad with hate and misery. He's ready to suspect anything and anyone."

She sat down again in her chair. Her bottom lip was drawn in and she was biting it between her teeth. James Wilson knew that she was wishing now she had not told him about the hut. She had told it to save her brother from the risk of having Bond find him. And now that Bond had come back, she had told it for nothing.

James Wilson knew that whatever happened he would have to go up to that hut as soon as it was light. She had told him, and he could not erase the knowledge from his mind. He would have to go up. That was his job and his duty. All right then. It simply meant taking the gun away from Bond. That was all. That was all.

"Couldn't you get that gun away from him?" She came right into his thoughts.

"I might. I'll do something. I promise that I won't let him touch your brother. I promise you that."

"But what will you do? You'll have to get the gun away from him."

"Yes. I'll do something, anyhow."

"It . . . it mustn't happen like that. Please. Please."

"It won't. I swear to you it won't."

Then they heard the latch of the front door again, and they knew that Bond had returned from looking at the barn.

This time he stamped his feet in the hall to knock some of the loose snow off. Then he came slowly into the room. It was clear at a glance that some of the spike had gone out of him.

"There was nobody there," he said.

They did not answer him. James Wilson could see that he was very, very tired.

"Well?" Bond asked him, rallying himself. "Haven't you got any suggestions? What are you going to do now?"

"I'm going to wait until the morning. There's no chance of finding anything tonight." He was hoping now that Bond would again take the search up on his own. But he knew it was a vain hope.

"You going to wait here?" Bond asked him.

"Yes. There's nowhere else."

Bond looked at him and wrinkled up his eyes.

"I think I'd better wait with you," he said. It was hard to tell whether his reason was suspicion or just plain tiredness.

James Wilson turned towards the girl.

"I should go up, if I were you, Miss Maldon. There's no point in your losing any more sleep." He tried to speak lightly, hoping to hide from Bond the fact that she had anything more than a casual interest in what was happening.

She stood up. He was hoping that she would not raise the question of Bond staying there too. She seemed to hesitate. But she had taken her cue from him, and she walked towards the door without saying anything. He went and held the door open for her, and put his hand under her elbow as she walked through. When she was just outside the door, he slid his hand down her arm, and found her hand, and held it for a moment. He held it firmly, trying to squeeze a message of confidence into it. He was glad when he felt her hand answering his.

She went up the stairs, and he walked back into the room. Bond was still standing. His coat was white with snow.

"I should take your coat off and sit down for a bit," James Wilson suggested.

Bond nodded, and took his coat off, and took it out into the hall and hung it on a nail. He came back and flopped down in one of the chairs by the fire. He was very different from what he had been half an hour before. He seemed suddenly to be glad to be told that he could let up for a while. He needed it.

James Wilson sat down in the other chair. He was thankful that Bond had stopped the battery of questions. He wanted a chance to think.

He looked across at Bond, slumped in the chair a few feet away from him. The gun was still lodged in the crook of his arm. To take that gun away now was not in itself a very difficult problem. It would mean a scrap, but it should not be very difficult. But James Wilson knew that the thing did not end with taking the gun away.

He tried to get it all straightened out into a clear pattern in his mind. One point was certain, there could be no doubt about it. As soon as it was daylight, he would have to find that path and go up to the hut. There was no getting out of that. There could be no excuse for putting it off. That was what he had to do, and that was simply that. And so, remember, he told himself, it is no good letting things slide until daylight. It is no good leaving this house in the morning with Bond and his gun by the side of you. Because you know what will happen. You promised her something, and you meant it as much as you ever meant any promise in your life. You meant it because you wanted to mean it. You made the promise because you wanted to make it. It was something you could do for her, and you grabbed at it. You'd make it all over again, this moment, if she were here alone with you now. And if you leave this house with Bond and his gun by the side of you, what will happen when you get down the lane to the spot where the path begins? What will you do? Which way will you go? Your duty will be tugging you to find the path and get up it quickly. But your promise to her will be holding you back, making you fight for time, making you try to forget you know anything about the path, making you go straight on along the lane in the hope that somehow you can shake Bond off. If you let yourself get into that position, it will be a straight fight between your job and what you promised to her. And which will win, with you? No, that isn't fair. It isn't fair to think of it bluntly, one or the other, like that. Your job is your job, and if it stinks then it is up to you to throw it up, but not in the middle of something. Does that mean you would go against your promise to her, if you got in that position? Would you be prepared to face her afterwards, if anything happened, and to tell her that you couldn't keep your promise because you had to do your job? All right, why not? She's nothing to you. Nothing at all. You don't owe her anything. You didn't ask her to tell you about her brother. She told it of her own free will. She's nothing to you. She's nothing to you. Don't keep saying that, you fool. You know yourself well enough. You can't talk yourself out of it like that. She didn't tell you anything. It was just that the two of you shared something. That was what it was. That was the way it felt, anyway. And is that nothing? Don't wriggle, James. Is it nothing? No. It is very far from being nothing. You are only human, eh? That's an old excuse. But it's a real one, too. It's a bit late now to throw it aside. You didn't mind being only human when she was down here talking to you. When you felt that funny feeling of sharing things. When you wanted to comfort her. All the time with her. You were very much only human then. And tomorrow, down the lane, if you got in that position, and thinking of her, which would win? Your job is your duty. But which would win? Come on, face it. Which would win? Would you go up the path with Bond and take a chance? So that if anything happened you could never talk with her, and have that feeling of sharing things, never any more? Would you?

All right, you can keep it to yourself. You know what the answer is, inside you, but you need not actually give the answer because you are not going to get in that position.

And aren't you trying to pin a bit too much of it on to her? If it happened that way, the worst way, and Bond actually went the whole hog and shot him, and killed him, is it only her that would matter? What about you? Would it look good from your point of view? It would be the world's record bungling mess of a job, to say the least of it. So you don't need her as an excuse. You've got to keep this Bond in check apart from anything to do with her.

You could take the gun now. You could handle the scrap with Bond all right. But then what? That's the part that doesn't seem to fit nicely, the afterwards part. Back there in the snow, before you ever came near the house here, you toyed with the idea of taking it from him and you decided against. Never go back on a hunch. You were right then, and it still goes now. In fact it goes stronger than ever now. For one thing, if you forced it away from him now, he would know you were on the scent of something. At present his suspicions are only half-baked, and he might even sleep them off. But if you sharpen them up, by forcing his gun away here and now, then he may be still more difficult to handle. A gun is not the only thing that kills people. Unless you trussed him up, he might be worse than ever. And you cannot risk trussing him up. Suppose something went wrong. Suppose you got up to the hut, and you failed to make a pinch, and the chap got away. You could never talk yourself out of that one, if the only man available to give you any help had been carefully trussed up by you.

It was going to be so easy, an hour or so ago. If Bond had not come back tonight, it was going to be so easy. Once I had the fellow collared, Bond would have been all right. It is only in the heat of the search and the chase that he is likely to do something. He wouldn't shoot when the fellow was already collared. I could see to that all right.

James Wilson pulled himself up with a jolt. It was no good dreaming of how easy it might have been. He had to make his mind up some way or other.

He looked at Bond, slumped there in the other chair. His head had fallen forward so that his chin was supported on his chest. He was breathing deeply and heavily, nearly asleep. He was tired right out, and the warmth of the fire was acting on him like a drug.

James Wilson looked at him and his mind grasped at the sudden possibility. Sleep might be the answer. It might be as simple as that. If Bond was as tired as he looked, as tired as he ought to be, then he might sleep for hours. Two hours should be plenty, anyway. That was not long for a man to sleep.

It seemed a ridiculously easy answer. And then James Wilson remembered that it would not be light for nearly another three hours. She had said that he would not be able to find the path in the dark. But it would be worth trying. His eyes were good in the dark. It was too much of a chance to be missed.

He put his hand round to his hip and pulled out his half-bottle of whisky. He did not think Bond was properly asleep yet, and he wanted him to sleep as heavily as possible. He leant across and tapped him on the knee. Bond started. He had been very near to sleep.

"We're both of us pretty well soaked to the skin," James Wilson said. "Could you do with some hot whisky?"

Bond blinked his eyes.

"Have you got some?"

"Yes. I'll get some warm water."

"Don't trouble. It's all right as it is."

"It'll do us more good if it's warm," James Wilson said, and walked towards the door without giving Bond a chance to argue about it.

He found his way along the passage to the kitchen. He did not make much sound because his shoes were still off. He found an oil stove on the table, and he lighted it and put a little water in a saucepan on top of it. Then he found two cups. He poured a stiff measure for Bond, and a small one for himself. He brought the water nearly to the boil, and filled Bond's cup with it. Then he fiddled in his waistcoat pocket and brought out some aspirins. He broke two of them up, and dropped the pieces into Bond's cup. He had never tried them that way, but he thought the whisky would hide the flavour. If not, he could put it down to chalk in the water. He waited till the aspirin had dissolved, and then carried the cups back into the room.

"Here you are." He held it out to Bond.

Bond grunted his thanks. They both sat in their chairs and started drinking.

"Strong one," said Bond.

"We need it. No good catching cold."

"What's the time?"

James Wilson looked at his watch. It was nearly five o'clock.

"It's about half-past three," he told Bond.

Bond sipped the hot whisky steadily. When he had finished it, he put the cup down in the hearth. He still held the gun close to him. James Wilson put another log on the fire, and spread one of the blankets over Bond.

Already Bond's chin was resting heavily on his chest again. His whole body seemed to be stretched out and relaxed, as if longing for sleep. James Wilson sat and watched him. His breathing became heavier, more regular. On top of the tiredness, the warmth and the whisky and the aspirin were doing their work.

The heavy, hovering silence settled across the house again. It was broken only by the deep, steady breathing noise that Bond made. James Wilson sat and watched him carefully. He felt sure that once Bond got properly into a sleep he would stay there for hours. But he did not want to make the mistake of moving before Bond had gone soundly off. Sleeping in chairs was not the same as sleeping in a bed. Most people had a preliminary period. The relaxation of being asleep would let their heads fall sideways, and that would wake them up. He wanted to wait until Bond had got that part over. If Bond should wake up just at the moment that he was creeping out of the room, the trouble would start all over again, and worse.

He waited for over half an hour. Bond appeared to be really settled. He looked as if nothing would wake him. James Wilson glanced at his watch again. It was half-past five. With any luck, assuming he could manage to find the path in the dark, he could be up at the hut by daylight, and could have everything neatly under control while Bond was still sleeping.

He eased himself slowly and carefully up from the chair. He picked up his shoes from the hearth, and took his coat from where it was still hanging at the corner of the mantelpiece. Softly, soundlessly, he stepped across the matting of the floor. He had left the door into the passage half-open, and he could just pass through sideways without risking a possible squeak from moving the hinges. He stopped in the passage and put on his coat. Still carrying his shoes, he went across to the front door, and started to lift the latch, very slowly, a fraction of an inch at a time. It was binding rather tight against the socket, and when it finally came undone, it did so with a jerk. The sound was only tiny, but it seemed to James Wilson like a deafening crash across the silence. He stood still, listening for a moment. He could hear Bond's heavy breathing just the same. He slipped through the door into the porch, and closed the door behind him as quietly as he could. This time he stood listening for several minutes. He could not hear the breathing from where he was now, but there was no sound to suggest that Bond had woken and had missed him.

His feet were soaked and freezing now from standing in the snowy-wet porch in his socks. He put on his shoes and set off along the lane towards the barns. The snow had stopped falling. The clouds had started to break in patches, and here and there he could even see stars peeping through. Everywhere round him was white, thick white, and the clean surface picked up what little light there was from the sky and made the most of it. As his eyes adjusted themselves to it, he began to feel confident about finding the path. The snow relieved the darkness so that it was no more than half-dark.

He picked his feet up high as he went through the thick snow along the lane. There were plenty of tracks between the house and the barns. There were his own earlier ones, half-filled but still quite visible, and the recent each-way tracks that Bond had made. He picked his way carefully, setting his feet into Bond's deep footprints. His own marks showed inside the slightly larger ones made by Bond, but it was far less obvious than if he had made entirely fresh tracks. He was not expecting that Bond would follow him yet, but it was just as well to make it as difficult as possible.

He came to the point where the footprints turned off the lane to the gate that led to the barns. This was the point where she had said the path started, on the other side of the lane. He stood there with his back to the barns, while his eyes tried to search through the whitened darkness. The breaks in the clouds were bigger now, and the blackness in front of him gradually started to take a little shape. Against the sky he could make out the vague contour of the hill in front of him. Somewhere high up there was the hut, and the man he had got to find. A kind of curving knife-edge of ground, she had said. He wrinkled the muscles round his eyes as he strained to make out the shape of the ground. It was gradually, slowly printing itself in front of him. The whiteness seemed to take on different shades and shapes and distances. He could make out a row of straight dark lines, the leeward sides of the trunks of a row of trees. And just to the left of them, the whiteness seemed to be raised from the whiteness on either side. He fixed his eyes there, and kept them there, and it did not go away but became more definite as he stared. That was the beginning of the path, he was sure. That was just like what she had described.

He started to make his way towards it. It was more of a staggering clamber than a walk. Between where he stood and where the ridge started, a depression in the ground had been filled and effaced by the snow, and as he blundered into the drift his legs sunk in until the, snow was round his thighs. He had to dig forward with his hands before he could lift his leg clear to lunge forward again. The snow in the hollow there was soft and lightly packed, and every yard seemed to take him deeper in. He was floundering and gasping. When he fell, the snow seemed to tower up beside him, and he started to doubt if he would ever get through. It had taken him half an hour to cover a distance of barely thirty yards.

And then, quite suddenly, the snow was shallow, and he felt the ground firm underneath it. He paused, to get his breath back after the floundering he had done. Now he was nearer to the rising ground, and he could see quite distinctly, curving upwards ahead of him, the peculiar knife-edge of ground that she had described.

He felt with his feet for the narrow path, and started to walk up it. The snow on the narrow ridge was only an inch or two thick. His progress was very much easier now. He was having to watch very carefully where he stepped, for the crest in places was barely a foot wide, with a sharp, deep drop on either side. He went on steadily, climbing gently all the time, and curving gradually round to the left. He was getting on well, and he paused for breath and peered up ahead, wondering if he was getting near to the level ground where the hut was. But he could see no sign of any level ground. All he could see was that the path got very much steeper. He pushed on again, and soon he could feel himself leaning sharply forward against the slope of the path. The snow was binding on his shoes and forming into lumps of ice, and as the path got steeper it was hard to make his feet grip properly. He stopped and chipped the ice off the heels of his shoes with a penny, but it formed again before he had gone more than a few more steps. It was steeper now, steeper every yard, and he began to steady himself by leaning forward and putting his hands into the snow. The ground beneath the snow was very hard in places. It felt like rock. The snow would not grip on to it at all. He was turning his ankles sideways, trying to get a grip by digging the sides of his shoes into the layer of snow. For each step forward he had to test his foothold. It was getting steeper all the time, and every few steps he was losing his grip and slithering back a yard or two. He was hardly making any progress now. He was clinging to the slippery path with his feet and his hands and his knees, moving upwards a few inches at a time. The path was very narrow, barely a foot across. Each side, the ground dropped sharply down into drifts of snow. He began to wonder if this really could be the path she had meant. But there surely could be no mistake about this strange formation of the ground, this high, narrow curving knife-edge.

He turned his head to peer downwards, backwards, trying to see how far he had come. As he twisted his body, he felt his feet slip sideways. He threw his weight forward quickly to steady himself, but as he did so, one foot went off the edge of the path. It seemed to go plunging down into nothing, and the weight of it slewed his body round, pulling the other foot after it. He felt a sudden hard pressure across his stomach as it sagged against the edge of the path. His face was pressed down against the snow, and his hands and his fingers were clawing at it, and his feet and his legs were nowhere. He dug his fingernails viciously in. He could feel the pressure of the edge of the path move slowly up his stomach as he slipped backwards. The pressure came steadily, sickeningly upwards. It left his stomach and started to press against his chest. He seemed to be perfectly still, but there was the pressure of the edge of the path moving slowly up his body all the time. Although he did not seem to be moving, that shifting pressure told him that he was slipping all the time. His knees were resting against the side, but his feet were still nowhere. He did not dare to move them, to search for a hold, because he knew that the slightest movement would make him slip faster. He clung there, stiff and still, simply digging with his fingers and nails until his hands were trembling. And all the time the edge of the path was pressing higher up his chest.

He seemed to hang there for ages. He forgot about the hut and the path and Bond and everything else. All he could think about now was his fingers, pressing his fingers, digging them, straining them, trying to make them grip on that slippery surface.

The edge of the path came steadily creeping higher up his chest. Now it was across the front of his shoulders. It was squashing against his neck and choking him. It was under his chin, forcing his head back. His teeth were pressed tight together, and he shut his eyes and strained with the muscles of his neck. The edge of the path was thrusting his head backwards, and a singing came into his ears as he fought to hold his chin down. Only his chin and his arms were on the path now. The rest of his body was dangling downwards over the edge. His whole weight was held by the digging of his fingers and the pressure of his chin. He clung there, dizzy with the helplessness, waiting to drop. The buzzing in his ears became a deafening noise as he summoned all his strength into the downward thrusting of his chin. He waited for it. Another couple of inches, and then he would drop. One, two, three, four . . . the pounding in his ears was doing the counting for him. All he was conscious of was the pressing with his fingers, the straining with his chin, and waiting for it, waiting for it.

It was just about then that Bond woke up and found he was alone.

James Wilson stayed there, clinging and straining and waiting, as if it had been forever. And then, through the pounding in his head, came the gradual realisation that he was still hanging there, he was still in the same position, he was not slipping now. His chin had caught against a tiny ridge, and it lent just enough support to his fingers to hold him there.

He could not turn his head to look at anything. His chin was hard down against the ridge, and he had to keep it there. Very carefully and steadily he started to feel with his feet. There was snow banked against the wall of the ridge, and it fell away as his feet touched it, giving him no support. He started to work his feet gently up and down against the snow, knocking it away. The strain on his neck and the pressure under his chin were beginning to make things go black. And then he felt one of his toes against a hard, rough something that did not feel like snow. He fiddled carefully, found a toehold, and he flexed his leg and tested it. It was firm. It held his foot and all the pressure he could give it. With a hiss of relief he let the tension go out of his neck muscles. He lifted his chin off the ridge, and his foot still held.

Now he groped with his other foot, raising it a little, and found another hold, a few inches higher than the first one. Again he tested it gradually, carefully, and when he was sure it was firm he shifted his weight from one foot to the other. Then he groped with the first foot again, another few inches higher. Gradually his clawing fingers crept forward again across the path. He worked his feet steadily higher, until his hands reached right across the path and were able to grip the far edge. He fingered the snow away from the edge, and then his hands gripped firmly, and he lifted his legs sideways, one after the other, and lay on top of the path.

He lay resting full length for a while on the snow-covered slope. His chin felt bruised and his neck was aching, and now that he was able to rest it was several minutes before he could stop his fingers from trembling. The strain and the concentrated effort had brought his whole body out in a sweat, and as he lay still, the damp cooled quickly and clung chillingly against him. The wet of the snow was soaking through his clothes, and it mingled with the sweat so that he felt he was swathed in a blanket of wet coldness. He started to shiver, and he wanted to get moving again before the cold had a chance to strike into him, but his fingers were trembling and his arms were twitching, and he had to rest first. He turned his head and peered down the path, the way he had come, and up the path the way he had to go. He could not see the bottom or the top of the path, and he had no way of telling how much there was left for him to climb. But it looked as if it was going to be a little bit easier now. He knew it was really carelessness that had sent him slipping off the path. He peered down the side, to where he had nearly fallen. He could see that he would probably have dropped a long way. He would not have hurt himself, because the snow would have cushioned him, but if he had gone right down the side it would have been almost impossible to have got back up to the path. As he looked over the side, he knew he was going to be very, very careful for the rest of the climb.

He raised himself up on his knees, and started on upwards again. He watched himself carefully all the time, keeping exactly in the middle of the narrow path. He made no attempt at walking any more, but crawled up on his hands and knees, digging his toes in behind him. The slope was getting easier, but the extra care he was taking made his progress even slower than before. He crawled on, slowly and steadily upwards, and it seemed as if the path would never end. His trousers were sodden, and it felt as if his bare knees were pressing against the snow. His clothes were a heavy, dragging weight, and he was sweating again but cold at the same time, and he was tired, achingly tired, and the narrow white climbing path seemed to go on forever. He paused occasionally, resting for a moment or two, but each time he stopped he thought of Bond, and of all the time he had wasted dangling from the edge of the path, and he pushed himself on, crawling and grovelling upwards through the snow.

The slope was suddenly easier, and he got up from his hands and knees and started walking. The path was almost flat now, and widening, and the snow was thicker, and he found himself once more having to lift his feet up high to take each step. He remembered what the girl had told him. The ground was almost flat, and the narrow path was ending, and he knew he must be near the plateau where the hut was. He stopped, and peered round carefully in a semi-circle before him. It was just a solid mass of whiteness. And as he looked, it started to lighten. The whole scene was gradually becoming more visible and real. The skylines were sharper against the sky, and the vague masses of whiteness around him suddenly took on their shapes of hills and slopes and valleys. It was as if some hand had moved the focus of a lens. It was the dawn coming.

Now he could see where the plateau started, twenty or thirty yards further up. It was from there that he ought to be coming in sight of the hut. As he started to walk up the last part of the slope, he felt his pulses pumping a little quicker, and his tired muscles were pulling themselves into a taut preparedness. As he came up towards the edge of the plateau, he stopped for a moment to look back the way he had come. He could see, far below him, the valley where the farmhouse was, and he thought he could make out the top of the roof, peeping up from behind a ridge. It looked a long way down there, to where the white lane wound its way through the rest of the whiteness. The path behind him curved away and disappeared half-way down. As he stood and looked down into the valley, it seemed like a stilled, hushed world in which he was the only creature living.

It was because of the bend in the path that he did not see the tiny distant figure that was Bond, just starting to struggle his way up the lower slope at the bottom of the path, following the clear fresh tracks in the snow.

SIX

James Wilson came up on to the plateau, lifting his feet high over the thick snow. And then against the other whiteness, he saw the square white shape that was the hut. When he saw it first it was about twenty yards away from him. The snow had blown and clung against it, and from where he was standing there was no break in the whiteness of it, no door or window showing. He stood still, looking at it, looking for signs of tracks in the snow around it. There was nothing. From where he stood it looked desolate, dead and forgotten. He wondered if this was really the place, if she had told him wrong, if she had been mistaken. He started to walk towards it slowly. He could feel his pulses pumping, and the tiredness had gone from him and the coldness was forgotten. He came slowly nearer to it, yard by yard. He was half-way towards it, three-quarters of the way. He stopped, five yards short of it, and stood listening. There was nothing, no sound but the pumping inside him, no movement but his own breath on the air. He started to move round sideways, circling the hut. Keeping the same distance away from it, he went round three sides of it, and still there was no door or window, and no sign or sound. He moved slowly round the last corner, and then he saw the door. It was standing open, outwards. It had been pushed open from the inside, piling the snow with it as it came.

Still keeping his distance away, he came slowly round until he was opposite the door. The hut was small and the door was narrow. There were no windows, and the hut was dark inside. From where he stood looking, about five yards away, the inside of the hut was just a blank and empty darkness, a patch of nothing against the whiteness all around. His eyes were trying to pierce into the dark interior, but he could see nothing there. No sound or movement came from inside the door. He took a step towards it. There was still no sound. The silence and the stillness made his pulses start thumping again. It looked deserted, utterly deserted, except for the fact that strength had been needed to push that door open against the snow. He went closer to it, slowly, watching, his hands and everything ready. He was only a yard away from the door now. He was near enough to see inside. He could see two boxes, turned on end, a big one for a table and a smaller one for a chair. An oil lantern, unlighted, stood on the big one. The walls were dark, unpainted wood. He took another step forward. He was almost in the doorway.

The sudden sound made his spine jerk.

"Don't come in!"

He stopped, tense and rigid, almost in the doorway. The voice was high-pitched and threatening. It came from the dim half-darkness of the hut. And then, by leaning his head to one side, James Wilson could see him. He was crouched back against the wall in the darkest corner. His clothes were dark and his face was dirty, and against the wooden wall he hardly showed.

James Wilson looked at him, waiting for a moment. He wanted to let himself relax a bit before he spoke. He tried to make his voice sound casual and friendly. "Hullo, Danny," he said.

"Don't come in!"

And now James Wilson saw the glint of light that was a knife in Danny's hand. It was a long, straight-bladed knife, and he held it pointed forward, his thumb pressed down on the flat of the blade.

"Don't come any further. I shall kill you if you do." His voice was not threatening now. He was simply explaining what he was going to do.

James Wilson stood where he was. He tried to keep his eyes off the knife, and to look into Danny's eyes.

"What makes you want to do that, Danny? I haven't come to hurt you."

"You are one of the men who ran after me. There were a lot of men running after me."

"I should put that knife down if I were you, Danny."

"The men couldn't catch me. I ran too fast. They wanted to hurt me, but I ran too fast."

"I don't want to hurt you. Why should I want to hurt you?"

He glanced at the knife again. It was still held firm and pointing. It would take several strides for him to reach Danny. He would have to get a lot closer before he could start anything.

"I'm Danny," the boy said suddenly.

"Yes. I know."

"I'm Danny Maldon."

"Yes. I know you are." The knife was held steady and firm. It looked as if the blade was double-edged.

"Where are all the men who ran after me?"

"They're not here, Danny. You needn't worry about them. They're not here."

"I ran too fast for them, didn't I?"

"You did run fast, yes, Danny."

"This is my hut. It's mine. If you come in I shall kill you."

"I don't want to come in to your hut, Danny. I only want to talk to you. Why not come out of the hut, and talk to me outside?"

"No. You want to hurt me. You want to punish me."

"No, I don't."

"Yes, you do. You ran after me. All the men who ran after me wanted to punish me. They wanted to hurt me, too."

"But they are not here now, Danny. There's no need to worry about them."

"I ran too fast for them, didn't I?"

"Yes."

"They wanted to hurt me, but they couldn't catch me."

"No. They won't catch you, Danny."

"They couldn't catch me, because they were only running, and I was an engine."

"An engine?"

"Yes. I was an express train. And then I was a motor car. I knew they couldn't catch me."

James Wilson took another look at the knife.

"They won't catch you, Danny," he said. "They are not coming here." And as he spoke he moved one foot very slowly forward towards the inside of the hut.

"No! Don't come in!" The knife was jerked forward towards him at arm's length. Danny was quick and sharp, and the knife was jerked forward before James Wilson even had time to change his weight from one foot to the other. He drew his leg back again, and stood in the same spot he had been in before.

Danny suddenly pulled his arm back, and lifted his hand and pointed the knife straight at his own throat. "I'll kill myself as well!" he said. "I'll kill myself if you come into my hut."

"No, Danny! Don't do that. I'm not coming into your hut. Look, you can see, I'm not coming into your hut."

"I'll kill myself if you do. Perhaps that would be better, if I kill myself. Then nobody can ever hurt me."

"Look, Danny. I'm not coming in. See?" James Wilson took a half-step backwards. He was bracing himself ready to jump forward if it should happen. His eyes were fixed on the knife now. The knife was very close to Danny's throat.

Now Danny suddenly shifted his eyes, as if he were remembering something. Then he brought the knife quickly away from his throat, and pointed it out in front of him again.

"No, I mustn't do that. I promised I wouldn't kill myself. I promised her that."

James Wilson saw that the knife was pointed straight at him again, as stiff and firm as ever.

"Who did you promise, Danny?" he asked.

"If you come into my hut, instead of killing myself I shall kill you."

"Who did you promise, Danny?"

"What do you mean?"

"You said you wouldn't kill yourself because you promised not to. Who did you promise?"

Danny swivelled his head forward as if he had heard a question that did not make sense.

"Mary, of course," he said.

"Who is Mary?"

Danny drew himself up proudly.

"She is my sister. She's beautiful."

James Wilson inched his feet forward. It was hardly anything, and Danny did not notice.

"Do you do what your sister asks you to do, Danny?"

"Of course I do. She is beautiful."

"Your sister wants you to come down to her now."

"She is beautiful."

"Yes, I know she is. And she wants you to come down to her now."

"Mary looks after me. She is the only one I take any notice of. I always have to do what she says. I like to please her."

"Then shall we go down to her now? She wants you to go to her."

"No, I'm not going."

"But she wants you to."

"Oh, no. I'm not going. I'm going to stay in my hut here. I'm hiding."

"But there is nothing to hide from, Danny."

"Yes, there is. I'm hiding from the men who want to catch me and punish me and hurt me."

"But you want to please your sister, Danny?"

"Oh, yes. I like to please her. She is beautiful."

"You'll please her very much if you come down to her now."

"No. I don't want to go down now. I'm hiding in my hut."

"But she wants you to go down now. You always do what she says, Danny."

"Only when she says it to me. I don't have to do it when you say so. I don't take any notice of anyone else. She is the only one I take any notice of."

James Wilson inched a little bit forward again. The knife was still firm and unwavering. It did not look like being any easy job, taking that knife away.

"Mary will not be pleased if you don't go down to her, Danny. Let's go down together, shall we?"

"We can't go down now. There's a lot of snow. The path will have a lot of snow on it."

"But we can get down all right. I've just come up it."

"I came up before most of the snow. It was snowing hard when I came, but most of the snow has come down since I came up the path."

"It's not thick on the path, Danny."

"It's thick here. I've been sleeping. When I tried to open the door, I had to push hard to make it open. There was thick snow in the way."

"But it's all right on the path. We can get down easily. Then we can go to see Mary."

"Mary can't see. Mary can't see anything."

"I know she can't, Danny. But she wants you to go to her."

"Mary can't see anything."

"Come on. Let's go down to Mary now."

"Mary doesn't mind not being able to see anything."

"No. But she wants you to go down to her now, Danny."

"She used to be able to see things, but she can't now."

"Danny! Don't you understand? Mary wants you to go down to her now. She won't like it if you don't go down to her now."

"Will she be cross?"

"I don't know. I suppose she will. She wants you to go."

"I don't like to make her cross. She is beautiful, and I don't like to have her being cross with me."

"Then let's go down to her now, Danny." James Wilson inched

another little bit forward. He was still a long way from being within reach.

"But I want to hide in my hut here. I don't want anyone to find me. If anyone finds me, they will want to punish me and hurt me."

"Nobody is going to find you, Danny. Come on. Let's go down to Mary now. She wants you to go."

"Mary can't see anything. She doesn't mind not seeing anything. She was going to see things again, but she said she didn't mind."

James Wilson suddenly stopped worrying about the knife and trying to get nearer to Danny without him noticing, and trying to get the knife away. He was suddenly fastening on to what Danny had said. His mind flashed back to what Mary had told him. Sometimes Danny was normal, it went in spasms.

"She was going to see things again?"

Danny gave the knife a jerk.

"Don't come in! You're coming nearer. I shall kill you if you come in my hut."

"I'm not coming in, Danny. I'm not coming any nearer. What was that you just said? She was going to see things again?"

"If you come in my hut I shall kill you. I shall kill anyone who comes in my hut."

"What did you mean, Danny? What did you mean when you said she was going to see things again?"

Danny quickly jerked the point of the knife at his own throat, and then pointed it back at James Wilson again.

"I could kill myself or I could kill you. I could kill anyone. Nobody could stop me from killing them. But don't tell her. She would be cross."

"Talk about her, Danny. Talk about Mary. Was she going to see things again?"

"She doesn't mind not seeing anything. I heard her say that."

"What did she say, Danny?"

"She can't see anything. I make faces at her sometimes and she can't see me. Then I laugh."

"But is she going to see again, Danny? Is that what you said?"

"Oh, no. She was going to see things again, but she didn't mind. She wanted to stay and look after me. I heard them talking. I listen to lots of people talking. I listen outside the doors."

"What did you hear them say?"

"I hear them say all sorts of things. I like it."

"What did you hear them say about your sister seeing things again?"

"Oh, no, she isn't going to. She wants to stay and look after me. She likes me. She is the only one I take any notice of."

"But what did you hear them say? Who was talking?"

"Mary was talking."

"Who was she talking to?"

"She was talking to the doctor. I often listen to people talking to the doctor."

"And what did the doctor say?"

"He said about her seeing things again."

"What did he say?"

"Mary had been to London. That's a long way away. I haven't been to London. Mary has."

"And what did the doctor say?"

"Mary said my mother was dead."

"Your mother?"

"Yes. Mary said about her being dead."

"And what did the doctor say?"

"The doctor said about her seeing things again."

"Who? Mary?"

"Yes. She can't see anything."

"What did the doctor say?"

"He said Mary was going to see things again. They were going to do something to her, and then she would see things again."

"When was that? How long ago was that?"

"A long time ago. In the hot weather."

"Was Mary talking to the doctor?"

"Oh, yes. They were both talking. They talked a lot. I listened all the time."

"What did Mary say?"

"Mary said she didn't mind. My mother was dead, and she had to look after me. She said she could not go to London again, to have the things done to her, to make her see again. She said I would get into trouble in London. And she said if she went away and left me alone here, I would get into trouble here. Mary likes looking after me. She doesn't mind not seeing things. She likes looking after me. She is the only one I take any notice of."

James Wilson had forgotten about the knife and everything else. As the meaning of Danny's words came sinking into him, he was down in the house again, seeing her, hearing her, and feeling very insignificant beside her. He wanted to be with her now, this moment, to be able to look at her with this knowledge in his mind, to be able to talk to her and listen to her, to be able to sit and share this thing with her. Now in a way he was understanding half the things he had wondered about before. This in a way was something to do with that strange impression of beauty that had come from her, even in the dark, even at that first moment when she had opened the door to them and he could not really see her. This thing that Danny had said, it was nothing in itself, it was only part of something else, a glimpse of an inner loveliness, that made him, as he thought of it, feel small and rather ashamed of a lot of things. Suddenly now for him the world had people in it who did not bargain, did not calculate, who gave and did not ask. His own crude world of move and counter-move was a worthless, soiling place, and he wanted to go to her, softly humble, and sit with her and ask if there was anything he could share. He had known about her all the time, in some way or other, he had felt it shining out of her, and he had loved it all the time. But you, he mocked himself, you don't properly believe things till they are put on a plate in front of you. You have trained yourself to be looking all the time for the ifs and buts. If you had not suddenly learned this, would you have found it in her just the same? Yes. Yes. But without the evidence, without the concrete something to grab hold of? Yes. You did. Why try to cheat yourself, why black yourself worse than you have to? You knew it was there in her all the time. And Danny saying this was just an extra glimpse inside her. But it helps. There's no harm in it helping. It helps to make you sure you are not just weak in the head for some peculiar reason. It's like a ripple on the surface of a placid pond. It shows you it's real, and not just glass.

He wanted to be with her now, this moment, now, to know it and to be with her.

His eyes were still facing across the hut at Danny, but his seeing was far away, down in the valley, in the house where she was, in the room with the fire and her sitting in the chair, and the firelight glinting on the copper of her hair, and her walking across the room, and then out in the kitchen preparing things to eat and drink, he thinking again of the cleverness, the difficulty that was somehow made to seem as if it was not there, the placid composure, no awkwardness, none of the things that might have been there and were so much better for not being. He was seeing it all again now, and hearing her voice, soft, haunting soft, lilting and flexing the words to mean so much more. And now with this sudden knowing about her, the new things that he had not known before, he felt something full and deep sweeping over him, dragging at him and hushing him, a feeling of wanting to hurry forward on careful tiptoe.

The sudden jerking of Danny's knife brought him back to where he was.

"You're coming in. Don't you come in my hut, or I'll cut you!"

"I'm not coming in, Danny. I'm not going to hurt you." In spite of the knife, it was only with an effort that he could bring his thoughts back from where they had been.

"How long ago did that happen, Danny? I mean about your sister and the doctor."

"Don't you hurt her. I won't let anybody hurt her."

"Nobody wants to hurt her, Danny. Nobody wants to hurt you or her."

"Then why are you asking about her? What are you going to do to her?"

James Wilson instinctively spread his hand out, pleadingly. The knife jerked quickly.

"Don't you come any nearer. Don't you come in my hut."

James Wilson drew his hand back again. He stood quite still, looking at Danny. They were both standing taut and stiff, both ready. He waited for something like a minute before he spoke again.

"Let's go down to her, Danny. Mary wants you to go down to her."

"I don't have to go unless she tells me. I don't have to do what you say. She is the only one I take any notice of."

"But she couldn't come up here herself and tell you, Danny. You know that."

Danny shook his head. A cunning little smile spread over his face.

"I only do what she says. I know she can't come up here anymore. That's why I come here, so that she can't tell me things."

"But you like to do what she says, Danny."

"Oh, yes. I always do what she says. I have to. She is the only one I take any notice of."

"How long is it since Mary hasn't been able to see, Danny?"

"I don't know."

"Is it a long time since you heard the doctor talking to her?"

"That was in the hot weather."

"But when you heard the doctor talking to her, was that last summer, or was it a long time ago?"

"He doesn't come anymore now. He used to come a lot, before Mother died. Sometimes he used to bring another man with him. He was a doctor, too. I used to listen."

"When did your mother die, Danny?"

"When I was up here in my hut. When I went down, she was dead. I didn't see her anymore. They wouldn't show her to me."

"Was that a long time ago?"

"That was after Mary went to London with the doctor. I haven't been to London, but Mary has. Mary used to go to London when she could see."

"But when she went with the doctor, was that when she couldn't see?"

"Yes. The doctor came to fetch her. She couldn't see anything. I made faces at her through the glass of the car, but she couldn't see what I was doing. The doctor was cross, but I didn't take any notice of him. Mary is the only one I take any notice of."

"When she went to London with the doctor, was that before your mother died?"

"Yes."

"And after your mother died, then the doctor came to see Mary again?"

"He came a lot of times."

"And what did you hear him say?"

"I heard him say a lot of things. He talked a lot. He made Mary cry once."

"Why? What did he say?"

"He said about her going to London, because they were going to make her see."

"Did he say he would make her see for certain, Danny?"

Danny puckered his eyes, looking bewildered. "He said about making her see," he said again.

"Now, Danny, try to remember very carefully. How long ago was the last time the doctor talked about making her see?"

"That was the last time he came."

"And when was that? How long ago was that?"

"It was a long time."

"But how long, Danny? Was it last summer?"

"It was in the hot weather."

"But try to remember, Danny. Think. Think hard. Was it last summer that you heard the doctor talking? Was it in the last hot weather?"

James Wilson was talking quickly, and pressing his words, and he could see that it was beginning to do the trick. He was edging forward, inch by inch, covered by the conversation.

"Think, Danny. Think hard. Try to remember. How long ago was it?"

"How long ago?"

"Yes. Think hard."

"I am thinking hard."

"Think about when the doctor was talking to Mary. How long ago was that?"

"He said about her going to London. But she didn't go. She doesn't mind about not seeing. She likes to stay and look after me. There's nobody else to look after me. I don't take any notice of anybody else."

"But when you heard the doctor talking to her, Danny. When was that? When? When? Think hard."

"I am thinking hard."

"Think harder, Danny, harder."

"I am thinking harder."

James Wilson was half-way across the floor of the hut now. His eyes were fastened on to Danny's, and he was pressing with his words and with his mind, trapping Danny's thoughts, forcing the boy's mind away from the fact that the distance between them was gradually, steadily lessening. There was only six or seven feet between them now. Another yard forward, and then he would have a chance. The knife was still pointing straight at him. But the arm that held it was extended full length, stiffly and awkwardly, as a child would act a tableau with a sword. That was the chance, he thought. The arm is so stiff and extended that it leaves no margin for him. Until he draws his hand back, he has no flexibility in his arm. His muscles are all full-stretched, and he has left himself nothing to play with. If he keeps taut like that, you ought to be able to do it. The knife cannot jab forward any further, not an inch. He could flick his wrist, but that's all, and apart from that you have the safeguard that he would have to draw it back first. All right then, that's the chance, but get your tricks right, make sure you get your tricks right. His thumb is pressing on the flat of the blade, and the way his arm is, if he twists, it will have to be from right to left, it couldn't go the other way, and if he tries a jab the natural pressure would be downwards. If you go on top, over the flat of the blade, watching for the twist, then you ought to be able to get hold of his wrist before anything worse than the flat of the steel has touched you. It's easy if you are quick enough. A knife is no good in an arm that is stretched as taut as that. But you need to be nearer yet, about another yard.

He went on pouring out the pestering questions, and trying to fix his eyes on Danny's and at the same time keep an eye on the knife and the arm. It's just a pity that it's a double-edged blade, he was thinking. That's just one of those pities. As you put your hand over, at the crucial moment you had better try to keep your sleeve well down, covering the inside of your wrist. That is your danger spot, the vein on the inside of your wrist. It'll make you feel just a little bit happier if you know that your thick sleeve is pulled well down, covering that vein.

He edged another couple of inches forward. He was moving by swivelling on his toes and on his heels, without taking his feet from the ground. He still needed another yard. One lunging grasp was all he could hope to have time for. If he did it before he was just the right distance, he knew he would simply be asking for the point of the knife.

He went on talking quickly, pressing his words, pressing Danny's mind to think of answers. Another couple of inches forward. Weight on the toes, weight on the heels, another couple of inches. Now he took his eyes off Danny's for a moment, fixing them on the glinting blade, gauging the angle exactly. Go on, go on. Three more little twists on the toes and the heels, and then you can grab.

And then Danny suddenly realised what was happening. He suddenly jumped sideways, his back against the wall, into the other corner of the hut. His arm was still stretched out stiffly in front of him, and as he went sideways he slewed his arm round so that the knife was still pointing at James Wilson. He could not go far, but it was far enough. The two yards between them were suddenly stretched into four yards.

"You're coming nearer!" he shouted. "You're coming into my hut!"

The arm and the hand and the knife were starting to quiver. James Wilson stood still, his pulses suddenly pumping quicker. His eyes were fixed back into Danny's now.

"It's all right, Danny. I'm not going to hurt you. Nobody's going to hurt you."

"You mustn't come in my hut. I don't want anybody to come in my hut."

James Wilson moved forward a little towards him. He was well out of reach of the knife, and this time he too moved more obviously. Danny saw it, and the arm and the knife started to tremble more violently.

"No! You mustn't come in. Go away! Go away!"

"Don't be frightened, Danny. I'm not going to hurt you. Let's go down together, shall we? Let's go and talk to Mary. Mary wants you to go and talk to her."

"I don't want to go and talk to Mary now. I want to stay here. I want to be in my hut."

"You can come to your hut again, Danny. But Mary wants you to go and talk to her now." He took another half-step forward. His eyes were fixed in Danny's, but he could see that the knife was trembling uncontrollably.

"I'm not going. I'm going to stay here. And you mustn't come in my hut. Don't come in my hut."

"Let's go down now, Danny. Come along." James Wilson held his arm out.

"I don't want to. I don't have to come with you. Please don't come into my hut. Please don't come any nearer!" The threat had gone out of Danny's eyes, and they were pleading now.

"Please! Please, don't come any nearer. Please stay away! Please!"

"It's all right, Danny. I'm not going to hurt you. Nobody's going to hurt you."

"I don't want you to come in my hut. I don't want you to come any nearer. Please don't come any nearer."

"Come along now, Danny. Let's go down together."

"I don't want to. Please! Please don't come any nearer. Please!"

The knife was trembling violently now. James Wilson took another half-step forward. He knew it was over. He felt and knew his domination over the trembling boy in front of him. The threats had gone, and there was only pleading now, and fear, and trembling. The knife that wavered at him was useless and powerless now. He could take it now without a fight, without a grab. Just calmly and steadily he could take it away from him. It was going to be just as he had promised her. No hurting, no fighting, no nothing. He reached his hand forward, high over the blade.

Danny screamed then. And as he screamed, his eyes were not looking at James Wilson, but over his shoulder towards the door of the hut.

James Wilson jerked his hand back from over the blade of the knife, and in the same movement swung his head round to look at the door. He saw Bond, and he saw the two long barrels of the shotgun, and he saw the look on Bond's face. He jumped across the floor of the hut and grabbed the barrels with his hand. As he forced the gun to one side, the report of one of the cartridges firing made a noise in the tiny space of the hut that felt like someone punching his ears. The gun was pushed well aside and the pellets splattered against the wooden wall. Then the smell of the burnt powder came up and pricked the inside of his nose, and his eyes smarted, and all he knew for the moment was that he had the barrels in his hand and he was pressing them away and pressing them down, and his ears were hurting and his eyes were watering and what he had to do was keep pressing the gun away and pressing it down. He could feel it pressing against his hands, straining to come upwards, and something kicking against his legs and a shoulder butting against him, and then a voice shouting words right close to his ears, and then he shut out everything else and thought only of the gun and his hands gripping hold of it, and pressing, straining and gripping and pressing it down, keeping it down, keeping it pointing away. The shoulder kept butting against him hard, and the gun was straining to come up, it would not give way, it was going down an inch and then coming up an inch, losing and then winning again, and every time it tried to come up he was wondering what had happened to the strength of his arms. He went on gripping and pushing and pressing, and he was waiting for the second report, the second bang that would mean both the barrels were empty, but he pushed and strained and waited and still the second bang did not come. And suddenly the gun gave way, and the force of his own pressing sent him slamming forward, down on his knees and battering his head against the wall of the hut.

His forehead hit a shelf of wood with a dull, dizzing thud, and for a second or two the whole thing went hazy for him. Then he knew that the gun barrels had been snatched out of his grasp, and he turned himself round, sprawling on the floor, and saw the gun levelling up, and heard another scream from Danny, and saw Bond's legs in front of him, eye level, and he jerked his own legs out, and hooked one toe round behind Bond's ankle and then rammed the sole of his other foot against the side of Bond's knee. Bond went smacking over in a straight line sideways, clattering the gun down with him. James Wilson wrenched himself up on to his feet again, but Bond was up as quickly, leaning down to recover the gun. His hand was nearly on it when James Wilson landed on him with a clawing jump. The force of it carried them both to the floor, gripping at each other wherever they could find a hold.

They both had their coats on, and they sprawled together on the floor of the hut in a clumsy, uncertain grasp. The gun was lying on the floor, and they had rolled a yard or so away from it. James Wilson had landed on the back of Bond, and was struggling to find a good hold, but the bulkiness of the coats made it difficult. Bond's strength made it difficult, too. He was thickly built, but the thickness was muscle and hard stuff. James Wilson could feel his massive strength as they writhed and twisted there together. He was trying to concentrate on getting a good hold on Bond, and he was trying to look at Danny, and he was trying to keep an eye on the gun. It was too many things at the same time, and he suddenly felt the whole weight of Bond's body come swinging over on top of him, pinning him down on the floor and squashed his stomach so that most of the breath came gushing out of him. He tried to push Danny and the gun out of his mind as he wriggled and strained to shift that weight away from him and get round on top or get on to his side. What he wanted to do was to reach the trigger of the gun and let the other barrel off. That would be a start, anyway. It was not going to be safe for a moment until the other barrel had gone off. When he had done that, perhaps he could stop to think. But the gun was a yard out of reach, and this Bond was going to take a bit of holding. He was still on top, and he was going to take a bit of shifting.

Then there was a whooping noise from Danny, and James Wilson flicked his eyes across the back of Bond's shoulder and he could see the boy dancing about, hopping up and down, clapping his hands delightedly, and then he heard him shouting at them, urging them on to have a good fight. He was jumping up and down in his enjoyment of it, and clapping his hands together, and one of his hands still held the knife, and the thought went through James Wilson's mind that at any minute he would cut his own hand off if he didn't stop clapping. And then James Wilson gathered himself and gave the hardest wrench he could find, and managed to twist himself from under that pulping weight, and on to his side, and he clapped an arm quickly across over Bond's chest and felt for his left arm to put a strainer on him, but the coats got in the way again and he muffed it, and then they were rolling over together again like a couple of hugging bears, and he was trying to get a hold on Bond and trying to figure the other things too and it was all too many things. Bond was on top of him again, and he came down with a sickening bump, and he knew he was making a mess of things because he could not concentrate on Bond, because he was trying to do Bond with his body and leave his mind for Danny and the gun. He was making a mess of things fast, and it suddenly swamped across his mind what a mess of things he had made already. It was all just wrong, and it could have been all just right.

Get off for God's sake, he thought himself saying. Get your weight off my belly. For God's sake get it off. *Get it off!* If only you could get at that gun and squirt the other barrel, that would be something. That would leave a breathing space for someone. But it's all mucked up now. He is dancing about there and clapping his hands, and he'll have his fingers off in a minute. By the sound of his cackles, he has just struck one of his worst patches. She said he went in patches. It's mucked up now all right. You had him where you wanted him. You were right on top of him, you had him beaten, you could have taken the knife and taken him without even a scrap. But now he's snapped out of the place you put him in. He's not the same soft putty any longer. Somebody's going to get hurt now. Somebody. Take your weight off. Take it off! He managed to snatch an arm free, and he brought his elbow over sharply and it got Bond on the side of the neck and he heard a grunt and then the weight was easier and he wriggled out and then they were rolling again.

Danny clapped harder and his cheers were louder as they rolled together across the floor. Danny liked the rolling parts. He hopped up and down with delight as he watched them. James Wilson caught another glimpse of the knife flashing in his hand, and as he rolled and struggled with Bond his strength was being spoiled by the rising temper that he felt against himself. He knew he was fighting the wrong man. He had let the whole thing get so mucked up that now he was fighting the wrong man while the one he was after danced and watched and clapped. Things seemed to be sensible step by step, and then suddenly you took a bird's eye view of the whole situation, and it was upside down. And remember you have a job to do, he told himself suddenly, fiercely. Remember what it is you are doing, supposed to be doing. He may be someone's brother, but you cannot hang up because of that. Remember the other things. Remember who that is, dancing around there. Remember what he has done. Remember who you are. And now look at you, struggling on the floor with the wrong one. The temper against himself was welling up inside him, and it was the wrong kind of temper, the kind that makes you miss your holds and muff whatever you are doing.

And then he saw Danny stoop down, and pick up the gun, and as the weight of Bond rolled on top of him again he saw Danny standing over them waving the knife in one hand and the gun in the other, and his hand was somewhere round about the trigger. And then James Wilson went to work.

He was underneath Bond but the weight was on his chest, and he found room to bend his knee and slide his leg upwards, and then for a moment he slackened everything in him, and collected it all for a jerk from the hip, and he heard the air suddenly hissing out of Bond's mouth as the knee jabbed into him. Bond raised himself up quickly, his hands now pressing on James Wilson's arms and pinning them down to the floor. But the raising up just gave James Wilson the room to double his leg back still further and to put his foot where his knee had been, and then he lunged out with the full strength of his leg, and Bond went backwards, right into the air, and came down hard on his seat against the wall of the hut. James Wilson was up on his feet before Bond landed, and he twisted round and dived at Danny without waiting to judge about the knife or the gun. He dived straight for his legs and hoped for the best.

Danny saw him coming, and gave out a little squeal. He stepped back quickly. James Wilson had not waited to judge it properly, and his hands missed Danny legs by several inches, and he landed stretched out full length on the floor with his hands grasping at nothing. Danny squealed again as both James Wilson and Bond got to their feet at the same moment. He dropped the gun clattering on to the floor, and turned for the door and went dashing out through it.

James Wilson started instinctively after him, but he pulled himself back as he thought of the gun on the floor. He bent down and grabbed at the gun just as Bond came across the hut. Bond grabbed at it too, and they tugged it between them. The gun was at right angles between them, and James Wilson got his thumb through the trigger guard, and as they both tugged it he squeezed with his thumb, and again there was that feeling of someone punching his ears as the second cartridge splattered across the tiny hut. He felt the gun kick, but Bond still had hold of it, and James Wilson suddenly took his right hand off it, and bunched his first and drove it hard into Bond's stomach, and again there was that hiss of air out of Bond's mouth, and then the gun came free in James Wilson's hand and he turned and ran out of the door. As he lifted his feet high for the snow, he took hold of the gun by the end of the barrels and flung it sideways, sending it curling through the air, carried far by its own weight. He thought and hoped it had gone over the edge of the little flat plateau.

He could not at once see Danny, but his footsteps were deep and plain, and he went bounding along their track with all the speed he could wrench out of himself. His mind was clear now, and he knew that the one thing he had to do was to catch up with Danny. The boy could not have had more than a couple of minutes start. He could not be far ahead in this thick snow. He was sure to see him in a moment. The hills climbed again above the plateau, and Danny was only out of sight behind one of the ridges. His tracks were clear this time and he could not get away. James Wilson went forward along the tracks with long bounding strides.

And then Bond caught up with him, he was bounding there beside him, and a moment later he was actually creeping ahead. James Wilson whipped himself forward. What's the matter with your legs? he urged himself. Bond has just had it twice in the stomach, you heard the air come out each time, and yet you let him overtake you. What is the matter with your legs?

Bond had not troubled to retrieve the gun. He was only intent on catching up with Danny now. He shouted back over his shoulder.

"Don't think you're going to stop me!" he shouted. "Nobody's going to stop me!"

James Wilson dug down for his strength and his speed, and he was keeping up with Bond now. But he could not close the few yards gap between them. The snow was deep, and to run at all was a tiring, straining thing. He wondered if Bond was feeling it the same. And where was Danny? Then James Wilson remembered about that other chase, across the fields, before Danny had pinched the car. Danny had been winning all the way then, leaving him behind with every step. James Wilson remembered it now and knew that it was not going to be easy.

He pounded along behind Bond, and then suddenly they could see Danny. Then James Wilson knew for certain that it was not going to be easy. Danny was way out ahead, and climbing upwards, up the hills that rose sharply above the plateau. He was more than two minutes ahead. He must have been gaining all the time. And now he was climbing up a steep slope as if it were the easiest path he had ever tried.

Bond could see him, too, and the sight seemed to pump fresh energy into him. His speed increased, and it was all James Wilson could do to prevent the small gap between him and Bond from lengthening. He was having to admit to himself that Bond had a lot more strength and stamina than he had given him credit for.

The ground was sloping very sharply, and the going was getting slippery. They were all three following the same tracks, and as the ground became steeper James Wilson realised that in third place he was going to have the hardest job of all. Danny had fresh snow in front of him, but by the time he and Bond had both trodden it down and slithered on it, the path that was left behind them was harder still. The peculiar knife-edge of ground was continuing upwards from the plateau, and the path Danny was taking was too narrow to allow James Wilson to choose a separate parallel path. He had to follow in the mussed-up snow, and already he was beginning to slip and flounder, and inch by inch he was losing ground to Bond.

Danny was high above them now. The slope was getting steeper, really steep. It was clear that Danny knew his path intimately. He had chosen a side of the hill that had been in the lee of the snow. It was not nearly as deep now as it had been on the plateau. The ground was becoming harder and rougher, and under the snow it felt like stone or rocks. They were all of them using their hands as well as their feet now. The ground was getting rough and jagged, and although it was steeper the footholds were better. Every time he felt a specially firm foothold, James Wilson snatched a look upwards. Bond's feet were two or three yards above him, and then a long way further up was the clambering figure of Danny. Danny was climbing very fast. He was gaining on them all the time. He seemed to be familiar with every inch of the way, and to be climbing straight up without finding it necessary to search for his holds. He is too damned sure-footed, James Wilson thought. He puts his feet straight into the niches without even feeling for them first. We are not going to catch him at this rate. He's like a deer or a goat or whatever the things are. His feet and his hands must have suckers on them. He just goes straight up without troubling. Or is it that? Is it really that? James Wilson had to pause a moment to get his breath, and he took a more careful look at Danny. He saw the boy's foot slip, and he hovered for a second before he recovered himself. He glanced back and saw his pursuers, and then he seemed to go on faster than ever. James Wilson suddenly changed his mind. It isn't that, he told himself. It isn't just sure-footedness and knowing where the holds are. It is funk that is taking him up at that speed. He is taking a chance with every step, and he dare not slow down, he dare not even wait to check his holds. He is asking for it. The ground is steep and jagged, and if he slips, heaven knows where he goes to. All the same, he is good at it. He must have done it plenty of times before. James Wilson was finding it harder with every step, with every yard, and he was getting tired and he was having to flog himself. It was getting steeper all the time. It was not a path any longer, but a series of jagged rock ledges up the face of the hill. In places he could see the rock, where the snow had been rubbed right away by the two in front of him. He was sweating hard with the effort of climbing, with the constant effort of straining to keep up. The temper against himself kept trying to come back inside him. He was getting really worried as he saw Danny gaining all the time. He was getting flashes of doubt as to whether he was ever going to catch him. He began to wonder what he would do, what he would say. It was all that softening up, he told himself savagely. You had a job that simply fell into your hands, all neat and pat, and then you had to soften up, you had to forget the first lesson. He's a murderer, and you had him for the asking, but you softened up. And if you let him get away now, you will be for the high jump. And what if he gets away and does some more before you can catch him? He won't, by golly, he won't. You softened up, you fool, when it was murder you were playing with. Go on. Faster! You've got to get him. There's no room for any ifs and buts. You've got to get him. Go on. Faster! It's your own damned fault. The temper against himself was bubbling up inside him, and it drove him forward but at the same time it made his feet a bit less sure.

And then there was a yelp from up above, and as he braced himself and jerked his head up to look, he heard a shout from Bond. They both of them clung there, rigid and still, looking upwards. Danny was coming nearer, downwards. Slowly, steadily, he was coming downwards straight towards Bond. They could see him working desperately to regain his grip as he slithered down from ledge to ledge like a ball rolling slowly down stairs. Each time he seemed to hover and just fail to stay there. He was coming steadily downwards, straight towards Bond. The two men watched, fascinated by the helplessness of the slowly slithering figure above them.

Danny's feet were dislodging little showers of snow as he came, and the snow was falling down and hitting Bond in the face or on the chest, or skimming over his shoulder and hitting James Wilson behind him. A large, heavy lump of ice suddenly struck James Wilson on the side of the face, and for a moment as he recoiled from it he thought he had lost his balance. His feet just slipped an inch or two, then held again. The fear of slipping struck at him, and then he realised what a precarious position they were in. If they tumbled, they would bounce against the jagged ledges of rock, and tear themselves or smash themselves to pieces. Danny was not really tumbling yet. He was slithering slowly from ledge to ledge, nearly gripping but not quite gripping. And then the strange fascination of watching him suddenly finished, it snapped off, and the full understanding of what was going to happen came swamping at James Wilson. They were all three in a line, in the same tracks, going straight upwards. Danny was slithering steadily towards Bond, and Bond was exactly in front of James Wilson. Danny's weight would dislodge Bond, and James Wilson knew that his own footholds would not stand the slightest extra strain. He glanced quickly behind him, below him, and the sight gave him a stabbing tight feeling in his throat. He flattened himself tightly against the sharp ledges, and gripped the rock with his fingers until he could feel the edges going into his flesh.

"Look out, Bond!" he shouted. "Grip tight, or we'll all go down to the bottom!"

James Wilson felt his own hold as firm as he could hope for now, and he bent his neck back and looked upwards again. Danny was still coming steadily down, struggling and grappling furiously all the time to stop himself. He was now about ten or fifteen yards above Bond. But it was on Bond that James Wilson's eyes were fixed now. Bond had taken no notice of the shouted warning. He was standing up, not even using his hands to support himself. Instead his arms were stretched upwards, hands apart. With no care for what happened to him, he was waiting for Danny. James Wilson could not see his face, but even from the back, from the way his arms were stretched out ready to grasp, from the way his head was reaching forward, he could sense the fierce and uncalculating hate that was obsessing him.

Then there was a guttural noise from Bond, and he suddenly pulled in his arms and started gripping with them again. James Wilson jerked his eyes upwards again, and saw that Danny had stopped. He had managed at last to grip one of the ledges and hold himself. He was lying still, flat to the face of the rock, and the only movement was the heaving of his shoulders from the heavy breathing.

Danny had lost his long lead now. He was barely ten yards above Bond. Already Bond had started to climb again. James Wilson jerked himself into action, and pushed himself and heaved and grasped and wriggled his way frantically up behind Bond. The muddle was pounding through his head again. The one and only thing and the main thing that he had to do was to get hold of Danny. But Bond was between him and Danny. Bond was already clambering upwards again. If Bond got his hands on Danny . . .

James Wilson could suddenly see her. He could hear himself speaking. He could hear himself promising her. It won't happen like that. She asked, she pleaded, and you promised her it would not happen like that. You promised her it would be done without any fighting or shooting, without anybody hurting anybody. Well, there isn't going to be any shooting. The gun is down the hill there, buried in the snow somewhere. That was all you promised actually. No shooting. And that is all right, that is fixed, because the gun is down the hill there. You promised there would not be any shooting, and there will be no shooting. That is what you promised, isn't it? No it isn't. You are just trying to hide behind the details. You promised Bond would not get him. What you promised was that you would keep Danny safe from Bond. Then go on, damn you, damn your legs, what is wrong with your legs? Get up after Bond and stop him. You know what he is going to do. You could tell from the way he looked just now, when he stretched out his arms. Get up and stop him. Faster. Bond is going faster than you are. What is wrong with your legs? Don't let Bond draw away from you. Keep up with him. Catch him. Stop him. If he gets much closer to Danny, he will be able to reach up and grab his ankle, and then God help everybody. The boy won't have a chance if Bond gets hold of him. Bond is strong and hard, and at the moment he is all hate. He will not care who gets it as long as Danny gets it. If it helped, he would kill himself at the same time, and wouldn't even know what he was doing. Get up after him. Go on. You are usually good enough for most people. What has happened to your legs? Go on, don't fiddle with your feet so much, don't take so much care about getting a safe foothold. Think about Danny instead of yourself. Think about her. No, think about Danny and Bond. Go on, get up after Bond. Catch him. Pull him back. Go on. Force yourself. Faster. Bond is climbing now with the same reckless speed as Danny. And there is not much between them. There is damn little between them. There is less between them than there is between you and Bond. Go on. Faster. If Bond can manage to reach up and grab the boy's ankle, that will be the end. That will be the finish. The finish of Danny and perhaps Bond as well, and maybe you too when they both come crashing down on top of you. Go on, what's the matter with your legs? Don't wait to check your footholds. Use your guts. If Bond can manage to reach up and grab his ankle, that will be the finish of everything, and bang goes your promise. Go on, get up and claw hold of Bond. You must not let it happen like that. It just must not happen. You've mucked it all up all the way along, you've got to stop it now. You don't often make that kind of a promise. Couldn't you just keep this one? Please let me stop it, he asked. Please let me keep this one promise. I don't often make that kind of a promise, with no strings to it. It was not just words, it was not just saying something. It was thinking things, and trying to share something. It was more than just a promise with words. By golly, it was everything more. It was everything there is. Please let me keep this one promise.

He bit his teeth together and the pumping breath came hissing through them as he clambered desperately faster up the face of the hill. It seemed to be almost vertically upwards. The serrated ledges of slippery rock were cutting against his knees and his arms. He knew that he was not getting the holds properly now. He was not waiting to test his feet, and he knew that he would slip the moment the luck went wrong. He knew it, but all he cared about now was catching up with Bond, he had to catch up with Bond and stop him from grabbing Danny, he had to catch up and somehow get between them, quickly, faster, because of the promise, because he could not let it happen that way. Nothing else mattered except he had to get up there, faster, and get between them and stop it happening, because of her, because of everything.

He lunged himself upwards, trying to get closer to those scuffling feet above him. And then his foot slipped, jerking his leg out straight, and for a hazy second he seemed to be hovering there, holding nothing, and then he felt an edge of rock come up hard between his legs, and he was strung there, catching his breath with pain, holding at nothing and suddenly sick with fear. And then he found something with his foot, and pushed, and then he was clambering upwards again, aching and winded and frightened but only knowing that he had to get on upwards, faster, he had to catch up with Bond and stop it happening. His breath was pumping deep and hard, and there was a pain around his chest as if he had on a wire waistcoat and the buttons were too tight, and a pain where the edge of rock had hit him under the legs, and there were pains in his arms and in his legs and everywhere else. But all they added up to was a driving, frenzied urge to strain himself faster and faster upwards. He could not pause now to ease his breathing, to ease the tightening restriction round his chest. It's now or never, he told himself fiercely. Get up there quickly now, because you will not have any more chances. Get up and get between them somehow. Buck up, it might happen any minute. No, it must not happen. You've got to stop it happening. Go on, damn your legs and damn your pains and damn everything. Grip this bit, jam your leg on that bit, shove your knee in that corner, now grab that edge, go on, grab it, to hell with slipping, go on and grab it, now the next one pull, pull harder, shove a knee in there quick, oh

God do be careful, no don't be careful, you can't wait to be careful, go on, grab that one, yes grab it you spunkless mucker it's only the flesh off your thumb, don't wait, there's the next one, go on, faster, you're getting nearer to him, you're getting nearer to his feet, now keep it up, faster, to hell with the pain and to hell with slipping, you've got to, you've got to, you've got to. It's the only thing that ever mattered, and nothing will ever matter so much as you've got to stop it happening.

He was wrenching and flinging his body upwards now with the reckless speed that Danny had risked before. He was putting all his effort into the raising of his weight, not waiting to test the holds first, but grabbing them and stamping on them and hoping for the best. Even the fear of slipping had gone from his mind now, pushed out by the one consuming thought of what he had to do. All the time he could hear Bond's feet scuffling just above him, and he kept jerking his face up to have a quick look. He was getting nearer now. The fierce and desperate effort was beginning to tell, and the feet above him were coming steadily nearer. And as he felt himself gaining at last, his confidence started coming back to him, ringing like a bell inside him, and the bungling feeling was swept away, and his movements were surer as a feeling of ability came into him again. He was going to catch Bond, and get between him and Danny. He suddenly had the feeling that the whole thing was in his power. He had got it mucked up, but now he was on top of everything. He could do it, he could handle it, he could rise to it all. He had not made a promise that he could not keep. He was going to do this thing, and do it properly. Nobody was going to stop him, not Bond nor anyone else. He felt his strength surging into him again as he struggled upwards and brought the feet nearer and nearer to him. He was winning now, and the temper and the bungling were finished.

Then Danny slipped again.

James Wilson heard a squeal above him, and looked up quickly. It was steeper above, and where Danny had been climbing it was almost perpendicular. James Wilson saw him hovering there, and then he tumbled. This time there was nothing slow or slithering about it. This time there was no chance for the other two to brace themselves against the slippery ledges. Danny slipped, and then fell smack for about ten feet, and hit one of the ledges and bounced off it like a rubber ball. The angle jerked him outwards, and as the two of them crouched there, rigid with watching, his body curved down through the air right above them. It fell right clear outside them, with its legs and arm flying. It hit the ledges of rock again several yards below James Wilson. It hit them with a plumping thud and bounced again and went on further down and further down. It was twisting and curving all the time and bashing different parts against the rock every time it struck. It started with a long squeal, and then there were short, sharp squeals, and then further down there were no squeals at all.

The two men crouched where they were, against the steep slippery face of the rock. They were looking downwards. Neither of them was moving. The urge to rush and strain and scramble was gone from them. They were looking down, a long way down, to where the black shape showed against the whiteness of the snow. They looked, and when they moved it was to check their holds and grip more firmly. They knew there was no hurry anymore.

They came down slowly and carefully. He was dead when they reached him. There were pink blotches on some of the ledges that they passed on the way down, and where he finally stopped the snow was patched with red in an untidy circle round his head.

James Wilson reached him first. He checked his heart, but it was only a formality.

Bond came behind, slowly and differently. He stood quite a distance away, and when James Wilson turned to look at him, there was nothing of the same about him. Bond's eyes were on Danny, and the eyes were not the same. There was a droop to his shoulders and a limpness in his arms, and his body was not the same. James Wilson could see that the whole thing was suddenly dead inside him. It was gutted out and finished.

James Wilson turned his back on Danny, and walked over to Bond. He did not know what to say. Bond was a big and rugged man, and he was strong but he was tired, and he was not the same anymore. James Wilson saw tears collecting in his eyes. Bond was looking at Danny, but he was not seeing Danny.

James Wilson stood looking at him for several minutes. The Bond he was looking at now was a man he had never seen before. He was a grown man with a baby's eyes. He was tired and hopelessly lost.

"There's nothing to do," James Wilson said at last.

Bond moved his head and looked at him. The tears had collected now. He was suddenly lost and he did not know what he was meant to be doing.

James Wilson went across and gripped hold of Bond's arm. He could see that everything had dropped out of him. He gripped his arm tightly, trying to bring him back. He looked at him steadily, and then he said, "There'll be somebody needing you at home, Bond. The best thing you can do is to go on straight back. Go on straight back. Go down the path and make for the village, and get back as soon as you can."

Bond looked at him, watching him speak the words, not seeming to understand. But after a minute he repeated the words that had penetrated into him. "At home," he said slowly, nodding his head. "At home. Somebody at home."

He turned his head towards Danny again, and then turned away with his eyes fixed on nothing. He stood there for several minutes, quite still, waiting for things to sink in. Then, without another word, he turned away, and went down to the plateau, and across the snow and on down the lower path.

SEVEN

It was getting towards the middle of the day by the time James Wilson left the plateau and started slowly down the path that led to the valley. Bond had been gone for an hour or two. James Wilson had stayed, delaying himself, knowing that he had to go down, but deliberately putting it off. There was nothing he could do for Danny. He could not bring him down the hill alone. He would go to the village and make local arrangements for the body to be brought down. It was not his job. His job was over now. All he had to do now was to put in his report and then he could wash his hands of the whole thing. There was nothing to wait for.

But he waited, lingering, putting it off.

He went back into the wooden hut, and sat on a box there and smoked some cigarettes. There was melting snow spattered all over the floor, and the splintered woodwork where the shot had peppered it, and all the signs of the scuffle with Bond. But it was not the scrap with Bond that he was thinking about.

There was food in the hut, and he nibbled at a biscuit from the top of a packet, and then he found that he was hungry and steadily ate them all. He munched them slowly, taking a long time, putting it off all the while. He was damp and cold and tired, but he did not really notice those things. As he ate the biscuits he did not properly taste them. When he smoked, he lighted the cigarettes mechanically. He sat on the box inside the hut, and his eyes were on the walls and on the floor and on the snow outside the doorway, and on the thin smoke that blew out from deep in his lungs and rose quickly in the cold air. He looked at everything and noticed nothing. He was simply putting it off.

At last he looked at his watch, and knew that he could not sit there putting it off forever. He got up from the box, moving slowly and reluctantly, and walked to the edge of the plateau. He stood for several minutes looking down at the distant rooftop of the farmhouse. Then he pulled his eyes away from it, trying to pull his thoughts as well, and he went to the top of the narrow path and started on the slippery journey down.

The snow on the path was flattened hard down, by himself and

Bond coming up, and Bond going down. The slippery surface made him go very slowly, sitting down on the steeper parts and using his seat as a brake. But now he was lowering himself gingerly, inch by inch, pretending to himself that it would be unwise to hurry. He was killing time and putting it off, and whenever he came to a slippery part he was glad and grateful for the need to concentrate on what he was doing. The slippery parts were difficult, but they were easy for his mind because they rested his mind from the other things.

It took him a long time going down, but it had to finish, and in the end he was standing again in the lane, opposite the barns. The air was suddenly warmer, and the snow had a different feel under his shoes, and as he stood there he could hear the first drip-drip of the thaw coming off the roofs of the barns. He was facing the barns, and it was left towards the village and right towards the farmhouse. Strictly speaking, it should be the village, he thought. The report, and getting the body fetched down, those are the things that come first, strictly speaking. Humanly speaking there would be a case for going to the house first, to tell her. But humanly speaking does not carry any weight compared with strictly speaking. You have to learn to put strictly speaking in front of humanly speaking. All right, all right, he thought, you can shut up about this strictly and humanly question. You know only too darned well where you are going first. It is just you're putting it off, that's all. But you know all right.

He turned and started to walk very slowly along the lane towards the farmhouse. His feet were quiet on the snow as he went up the path to the door. He stood for several minutes outside the porch before he stepped into it and tapped with his knuckles on the door.

She stood in front of the fireplace, her elbows on the mantelpiece, her face resting in her hands. It was a long time since she had faced towards him or shown her face at all. He was standing behind her, awkwardly, in the middle of the room.

"I'm not going to cry or scream or anything like that," she said at last. But her voice was tight, and even the words she used were forced.

He went across and touched her very gently for a moment on the shoulder.

She gave no sign of noticing his touch, no sign one way or another, neither acknowledging nor resenting, and he took his hand away again, and moved away from her and sat down on the chair by the side of the hearth. The silence between them was heavy and awkward to him now. Before, with her, there had been moments when nothing was said, and there was no need to search for things to say, because the silence then belonged to both of them. This was different now. This was her silence, her own and no one else's, and he felt he had no share in it.

"It was an accident," he told her again.

"Yes, I know."

"I tried, I did everything I could."

"Yes."

"I really did."

"Yes, I know."

Her voice was giving no importance to what either of them was saying, and he fell silent again, feeling that any words he said would be merely intruding on her.

She was still not turning her face towards him, and as he sat and looked at her he was conscious of how different everything was. It is like a game of something on a board, he thought. You are one of the pieces, and you have jumped a couple of squares, and now the whole picture is changed. It is just as if somebody jogged the board, and put you all in different positions. You were going to do something for her, and now you have failed her. Your promises came a bit unstuck. Not completely. Only in a way. But look at it how you like, they came a bit unstuck. So now, instead of someone she's depending on, you are someone who has nothing to give her. You are a stranger, and you have no positive meaning to her anymore. You are a negative thing in her mind, an empty place, a nothing, you do not belong in her presence and you have no meaning to her. And the other way round, she to you, has that changed too? Yes, that has changed completely too, because of the things that are over. You are through with this job. The whole thing is finished and practically wrapped up. You have nothing to do here anymore. You have no responsibilities now. You do not have to talk to her anymore now, because there is no information you want from her. You, James Wilson, sitting and gawking around with a blind girl because you think you can get a clue from her. That is over now. Do you realise that? he asked himself. Do you truly and completely realise that? This sitting and talking to her and being with her now is not connected with anything you have to do. If you linger now, and keep putting off the moment of going, there is no double game about it now.

What is happening to you? he asked himself suddenly. I don't know. But it just shows that nothing ever happened to you before. The way you feel, it shows that all right. How do you feel, then? It's a mix-up. It's just a mix-up of not being exactly nervous and not being exactly cocky and not being exactly anything. But it shows you, because the other things just made you feel with the surface parts of you. They made your spine tingle, or they made your eyes go misty, or they made your pulses jump a bit faster. But that was all. You didn't feel before what you are feeling now. You didn't use the same deep parts of you for doing the feeling with. Nothing has ever happened to you before. Myra was nothing. All of them were nothing. And when you were poisoned, and thought you knew you were dying, that was nothing. And when you were frightened that time in the boat alone, with the storm blowing up and the mast gone, so frightened that you prayed, out loud, actually speaking the words—well, maybe that was something, but it was nothing the way this is now. This is different parts of you doing the feeling now. This way, nothing ever happened to you before.

She suddenly asked him, "Did you speak to him at all before it happened?"

"To your brother? Yes." He was glad that she had spoken, and he jumped at it eagerly, hoping that her silence was eased and ended. But she did not follow up her question, and although he waited to give her plenty of time, he did not wait long enough to give the gap a chance to settle between them again.

"He spoke about you," he said.

She still did not answer. But now he could feel that it was different again, that she did not need the silence any longer, that she wanted him to talk.

"He talked all the time about you and what you had done for him."

She did not move except for taking her hands away from her face. She still did not turn towards him, and she still did not answer, but he knew that she wished him to go on telling her.

"He said that you were the only person be cared about, the only one he would ever do anything for."

He saw her nod her head very slightly.

"He knew all about it, Mary," James Wilson said softly.

She half-turned towards him now.

"About what?" she asked quickly.

"About you. About the—things you gave up for him."

She shook her head.

"No. There was nothing."

"He told me about it."

"What did he tell you? He did not know about anything, and there was nothing for him to know."

"But he told me."

"What did he tell you?"

"He told me about the doctors, and the question of your going to London."

She shook her head again.

"He did not know about that."

"But he did. He told me."

"How did he know? Did he say who told him?"

"I don't think anyone told him."

"How did he know, then?"

"He heard the doctors talking to you." James Wilson paused, then added bluntly: "Danny used to listen at the door every time the doctors came to see you. He knew all about it."

She was silent again for a little while, and then she spoke softly, to herself. "But he wouldn't have understood. He wouldn't really have understood." And then she suddenly asked him: "Did he know what he was saying? Do you think he really understood about it? Do you think he did?"

James Wilson hesitated; but not for long. Go on, give it to her, he was thinking. Give it to her for keeps. You have failed her in a way, but here is something you can give her. It is a lie, but no one can ever know. It is a lie, but if you say it hard enough it will stand with her forever as the uncontradictable truth. That gibbering idiot could not grasp a thing like that. He could never really understand a thing like that. He could never add it up and get an answer. To him it was just a bit of fact without any meaning to it. Making faces at her was just about his level of understanding. But give it to her now, go on. It's the kind of lie that once in your life you get the chance of telling. It's got no books to it, it gets you nothing, but it gives. You failed her up the hill there, letting him get killed. But here's a way of bringing something back to her.

"That was the one thing he really seemed to understand properly," he said steadily. "He spoke to me just before he died, and he told me. He knew what a lot you had given up, to stay here and look after him. He made it absolutely clear that he understood. And he knew what it meant to you."

Her face was turned towards him now. Her lips were apart as she listened intently, fastening on to the words he was saying. And when he had finished speaking, she did not say anything, she did not move, and he sat there looking at her, watching her. It has given her something, he was thinking. Yes, yes, it has given all right. Look at the smile playing round the corners of her mouth. Look at the light that is shining somewhere. It never did that half as nicely in the painting in the magazine.

The snow was thawing fast now, and the drip-drip sound had grown into a steady noise of water running from the gutters. There was a lot of snow to melt, and if it kept on thawing all the time he knew it would be several days before the roads were clear again. Getting back to London was going to be a wet and tiring business. He shivered at the thought of it. Then he reminded himself that he was already late in making his way along to the village and finding a telephone for putting in his first brief report. He would have to sleep somewhere in the village that night, and his clothes were wet and he had nothing to change into, and the walk to the village would be a slushing wet paddle, and he shivered again at the prospect.

He heard her coming along the hall. She had been into the kitchen to make a cup of tea. She came in carrying a tray, and set it down on a little table in front of the fire.

"Shall I pour it?" he asked.

"It's all right, thanks. I can do it."

He watched her as she did it, deftly and unerringly. She was calm and phlegmatic about things now. Even when he had first told her about her brother, she had managed to control herself. She had not given way to untidy emotion. As he watched her now he was conscious of some firm steady keel that steered her and held her and poised her all the time, in everything she did and in everything she said.

She held a cup of tea out towards him, and as he took it from her he felt himself shivering slightly. It's the sight of that hot tea, he told himself, like the way you always go goose-flesh while you are running a hot bath. Or perhaps it's just that these sodden cold clothes are going to get their way in the end. It's something like that. It couldn't be anything else, you idiot. Although it was a funny kind of inside shiver. You couldn't be kind of nervous in any way, could you? You couldn't, could you, eh?

He took a sip of the hot tea, and then he stood it down in the hearth as he remembered the whisky in his hip pocket. He put his hand round and started to finger it slowly out of his pocket. That will fix you if it is the wet clothes, he thought. A drop of that in the hot tea will be just what the doctor ordered. He held the flat bottle in one hand, and with the other fingers he started to unscrew the cap carefully and quietly. Then he leaned over and poised the bottle above the cup, and started to tilt it gently so that the whisky would run into the tea without making a noise. For a couple of seconds he felt like a schoolboy. And then it hit him, the whole thing hit him hard and sudden, and he felt his face flushing hotly, and he thought you bloody something, and then all the blasphemies and swears he could think of were jumping viciously through his head, all aimed at himself, and he sat there stiff all over, holding the bottle where it was. You bloody something, don't ever do that again. Don't ever, ever, ever do that again. Please, for the sake of everything, don't ever. It's like throwing dirt on something you love. It tears the whole thing to pieces, even thinking of it. Taking advantage. The fact that it was something that didn't matter only makes it worse. It makes it slighting. Please, please, don't ever do that again.

He held the bottle where it was, and looked at her.

"You wouldn't like some whisky in your tea, would you? I'm going to have some to warm me up."

"No thank you. I'm not cold. But you must be frozen and soaked through. You really ought to get your clothes off soon."

He poured the whisky into his tea. He raised the bottle higher, so that the trickle made a noise.

"Yes," he said, "I must be getting along to the village in a few minutes."

"You'll stay the night there?"

"Yes. You said there was an inn?"

"A small one. But they will have a room."

He sipped the tea, and felt the heartening warmth of it go creeping down inside him.

She said: "What will you have to report? What will you have to say?"

He answered very softly. "Not much. It's only a formality." He had been hoping she would not ask about it.

"Will they want to ask me questions? Will you have to mention me?"

"No one will want to ask you questions, no."

"But you will have to mention me?"

He did not answer.

"Did I do wrong in trying to hide my brother? Legally wrong, I mean."

"You did the natural thing. No one would expect you to do anything else."

"Not you, perhaps. But . . . would the law say that?"

"The law is a clumsy fool sometimes."

"You mean they will want to ask me questions?"

"No. No one will ask you anything."

"But you will have to mention me?"

"No."

She hesitated a moment.

"You should do, but you are not going to? Is that what you mean?"

He did not answer.

"Is that what you mean?"

He did not answer. She waited for several minutes before speaking again.

"I don't mind answering questions," she said. "I don't mind having the whole thing raked up. It can't hurt me. It has happened, and now it can't hurt me anymore."

"You won't have to. No one is going to ask you any questions."

"But you will have to mention me. You will have to say everything that happened."

"No."

"But you will. I want you to."

"Why? What do you mean?"

"If you hide all that, your report will not be a true one. You will risk getting into trouble yourself."

"No, I shan't. There's no need to start worrying about me."

"I don't want you to start messing your job up just out of kindness to me."

"No one will want to ask you any questions. There's no need for us to talk about that." His voice was suddenly curt and brusque because he did not want to talk about it.

She held her hand out towards him.

"More tea?" she asked.

"Thank you." He guided his saucer to her fingers. As she poured the tea, checking the level in the cup with the tip of her little finger, he was coaxing himself to ask the questions he wanted to ask.

"What are you going to do?" he started at last.

She lifted her shoulders.

"I haven't thought yet."

"Who else is there?" he asked.

"Who else?"

"What I mean is, you can't stay here alone."

"Don't worry about me. Please."

"But what are you going to do?"

"Don't worry about me. It is time you started for the village, isn't it?"

"Have you got someone to go to? Can I get in touch with anybody for you?"

"No, thank you. It is all right."

"But you can't be here alone."

"Why not? I shall please myself."

"I'm only trying to help."

"Yes, I know. Thank you."

He started to sip the new cup of tea. He knew that he ought to be getting to the village and finding a telephone very soon. And he knew that he would have to head back for London first thing in the morning.

"You'll go to London to see the specialist now, will you?" he asked.

"I don't know. I haven't thought yet. I suppose I will."

"Do they . . ." he hesitated, fumbling. "Are they optimistic?"

"They were."

"Why do you say it like that?"

"It is quite a time ago now. They put a lot of importance on to the time, the need for trying without delay. It may be different now. I don't know."

"It won't be different now," he said.

"Won't it?" She smiled slowly, gently. "Won't it?"

"No." He was conscious that his voice was pressing and urgent. "I know it won't."

"How do you know?"

"I just know it inside me somewhere."

The smile was lingering, playing over her face.

"D'you know something?" she asked.

"What?"

"You help."

"But I haven't."

"Yes, you do."

"How?"

"When you talk like that. It helps a lot."

He laughed at her now.

"You're too easy," he told her. "That wasn't help, it was only good intentions."

She shook her head.

"It was help," she said, "done up in a swagger box lined with tissue paper and tied with ribbon."

She turned her face full towards him.

"Have you got a beard, Mr. Wilson?"

"Of course. A long shaggy one."

"With mice in it?"

"Usually. They're on holiday at the moment."

"How tall are you?"

"Practically a pigmy."

"And bald?"

"Completely."

"With hair growing out of your ears?"

"In profusion."

"False teeth?"

"Gold and china alternate."

"Do you dribble?"

"Constantly."

She nodded her head gravely.

"All just as I thought," she said. "I've wonderful intuition."

"You missed something, though."

"What?"

"I've got pink and blue spots all over my face."

"Oh, those! I didn't like to mention them. I know my manners."

"You seem to know your James Wilson, too."

"Oh, yes, I think I know my Mister James Wilson."

He suddenly put his cup down in the hearth, and stood up.

"Look here," he said. "I'll have to do something."

"What do you mean? What sort of thing?"

"I'll have to do something about you. I can't just leave you here."

"Don't be ridiculous."

"But I can't. You'll have to go somewhere, or get someone to come and stay with you."

"What are you talking about!"

"Don't fence me off," he pressed. "You can't stay here alone, and you know it. Why won't you discuss it with me?"

"It's not the kind of thing I like to discuss with a short bald man with a beard."

"I'm serious, Mary, really."

"I know you are. I rather wish you weren't."

"What an extraordinary person you are."

"I don't think so."

"Why don't you want me to help you?"

She did not answer. She leaned forward in her chair and felt for one of the logs at the side of the hearth, and tossed it gently among the embers in the big open fireplace.

"Why don't you want me to help you?" he asked again.

She answered abruptly.

"Please stop it," she said.

"Why? What have I said?"

He watched her fingers tapping nervously against her knee.

"It's not what you've said. It's what you're thinking."

"What am I thinking?" His voice was challenging her now.

"You are going to spoil something. You are very close to spoiling something."

He looked at her, puckering his eyes up with trying to understand.

"I'm only trying to be helpful," he said.

"I know. I just don't want you to spoil something for me, that's all."

He said: "You'll have to tell me. I don't know what it is."

She suddenly jerked herself, and made a little laugh come.

"Let's forget it," she said. "I'm being silly."

"Tell me."

"It's nothing. It's just that you are starting to be a bit sorry for me.

I didn't want you to do that."

"I'm not." He spoke sharply to her. "I was just talking ordinary practical sense. Sorry be damned." He was curt, feeling suddenly heated and cross and not quite knowing why.

She clicked her tongue, against her teeth.

"Language," she mocked him.

He joined her laughing.

"Which one of us is being a fool?" he asked her.

She shrugged her shoulders.

"You choose," she said.

He glanced at his watch and knew that he ought to be going.

"I'm sure to run into something or other as soon as I get to London," he told her. "But I'll be back to see you as soon as I possibly can. Within a few days."

"No, you won't."

"Yes, I shall."

She shook her head quickly.

"You won't. I don't want you to."

He laughed. "I didn't know you had been asked," he said.

"There's no point in coming to see me again. I don't want you to. I shall not be here, anyway."

"Where are you going to, then?"

"Don't let's start that all over again, please."

"If one of us is being a fool, I choose you."

"Maybe. But there is no point in coming back to see me again. I don't want you to."

"Why not?"

She was silent for more than a minute before she spoke again.

"You said you had to get along to the village and telephone to London," she said.

"Yes. But . . ." He stopped as he saw her stand up and hold out her hands towards him.

"Come here," she said.

He put his hands to touch hers. She held them for a moment, and then leaving go of one of them, and holding the other firmly, she led him across the room to the door, and through the door and out into the hall.

"It's out into the cold, cold snow for you, Mr. Wilson," she said.

"I wish I didn't have to go yet."

"You'll be glad to get back to civilisation."

"No, I won't. I wish I didn't have to go yet."

"But you have to, and there it is."

"Yes," he said. "Yes. I have to. But I wish I didn't."

"I wish you wouldn't keep saying that."

"Why?"

"It's—it doesn't make any sense. It's a meaningless thing to say."

"It isn't meaningless. I mean it exactly."

"Then stop meaning it."

He laughed. They were standing in the hall, halfway between the door of the room and the front door. His hand was still in hers.

"You can't control your thoughts and your wishes like that," he said.

"You can stop them from running away with you, though. You can stop them from making you late. You're terribly late."

"Yes," he said. He knew he had to go.

"Goodbye, Mr. Wilson."

"It's *au revoir*."

"Goodbye. Won't English do?"

"I shall soon be back to see you again."

"No, you won't. Goodbye, Mi. Wilson."

"James," he said.

"James, then."

"I shall be back."

"No."

"Yes, I shall."

"Please stop saying that. Please."

"But I shall be."

"No."

"I am simply and definitely saying that I shall be, Mary."

"No."

"In about a week. Perhaps less."

"No."

"As soon as I can."

"No." She took her hand away from his. "No."

"But you don't . . ." he had to stop and swallow. "You don't quite understand, Mary."

She did not answer straight away. She stood with her head half-lowered. She was breathing more quickly.

"Please go now," she said.

"I am going now."

"Go on, then."

He put out a hand to touch hers again. She did not move her hand away, but he saw her lips squash tight against each other. Her head shook quickly.

"Go now," she said.

"Yes. In a minute."

"Now," she said.

His feet were heavy, and his legs did not want to move. He did not know what it was he wanted to say to her.

"I'm going now," he said.

"Yes."

"I really must go now."

"Yes."

She put her hand on to the latch of the front door, and pulled the door half-open. The damp air from the thawing snow came gushing into the hall. He put his hand to the door and gently pushed it closed again.

"Don't say that about my coming back to see you, Mary."

"Say what?"

"You know."

She did not answer him. She stood, her face lowered, and he wondered if she was trembling a little. He did not know what he wanted to say and he was not sure what was happening to him.

When she spoke, her voice wobbled on some of the words and it seemed to come tightly out of her throat.

"You don't know what you're saying. You're being such a fool."

"I only said I wanted to come back. Just to see you again. You don't . . . I don't think you understand, Mary."

Her face was right down and he was looking at the top of her head. She found the latch of the door again and pulled it open wide.

"Go," she said. He could only just hear the word.

He stepped across the mat and stood in the porch just outside the door.

"You don't . . . quite . . . understand, Mary."

She pushed the door slowly closed. He watched the gap between the door and the frame getting narrower and narrower until it was only six inches. She held it there.

"I know what is happening." He could only just hear her voice. "I know what's happening. You mustn't let it happen, James. You mustn't ever come back."

Then she pushed the door sharply shut, and he thought he heard the bolt slide home.

He stood there, very still, outside the door, for several minutes. He looked at the door but he did not touch it. He stood there, stiff-legged, the minutes going by. Then he slowly turned away and started to walk through the thawing wet snow towards the village.

EIGHT

There had been things to do, and it was over three weeks before he could leave London again. But at last he had cleared things, and got leave for several days, and with a strange kind of holiday feeling inside him he packed a bag and headed his car northwards. He started early, before the dawn, driving out of London with the streets completely empty, making good time and running through Baldock before he switched his lights off. There had not been any snow in London, and for a long way the roads were dry and he drove fast with his hands lightly on the wheel. He was driving his own small touring car, and as soon as it was light he buttoned his coat under his chin and put the top down. He loved to drive a long trip alone, and as the cold air pricked his ears he started singing. He pulled up at a coaching inn for breakfast, and the air had got right into him and he ate everything within reach. Four hours later, when he stopped for lunch, he was not far short of where he was going.

At the lunch-place they were talking of the snow that had fallen three weeks before, and of how some of the secondary roads just to the north were not properly cleared yet. It had thawed for a while and then hardened again, and in places there was still a lot of snow to go. They asked him which way he was going and he told them.

"You'll about get through there all right," someone said. "There was a couple of cars ditched up along that road when it first came down, so I hear. They do say one of them's still there. A fellow in here was saying that one of 'em was stolen and the other was some police chap chasing him. Rare old mix up."

Soon after he had started again, he came to the snow quite suddenly. It lay across the fields and was ridged up along the side of the road. He passed through the little village from where he had borrowed the other car three weeks ago. He had gone back to London by quite a different route, getting a horse trap to a railway halt away to the east, and this was only the second time that he had ever travelled along this road. Now he started to recognise it, and it gave him a sudden sense of getting near to where he was going, and without realising that he was doing so he eased his foot from the pedal and started to drive more slowly. But then he was starting the climb, and here the snow was still on the road, pressed down and half-melted but still fairly tricky, and he was changing gear and holding the wheel carefully, so that the handling of the car was taking three parts of his mind away. Then he topped the crest and saw what he had not been able to see the time he had done it in the dusk with the snow swirling, and he was quickly into bottom gear and gingerly humouring the car down the sudden steep hill where the snow still lay. In the ridge at the side of the road he could see the deep furrows where they had hauled the car out, and then a little further down there was the car that Danny had driven, still in the drift and looking as if it would stay there for a time. Then ahead and slightly to the left he could see the hill. It was still entirely covered with white up there. He did not want to think much about up on the hill, and he wished it did not have to be quite so near to where she was. Then he came to the narrow little lane that led down to the farmhouse, and he turned into it, pushing the hill out of his mind, and as he drove down the lane he felt a smile coming on his face although he was not even trying to put it there.

The snow still lay thick in the lane, but it was getting mushy and it was pressed down with several lots of wheel marks. He passed the two barns, and then he could see the farmhouse. He drove his car right up to the gate and stopped it there. He got out, squelching his feet down into the slush, and walked up the path to the door. His eyes were on the door and he knew that he couldn't stop smiling.

He rapped with his knuckles against the door, and stood there waiting. Then he rapped again, a little harder. He waited again for half a minute. There was no bell to pull, and when he knocked again he knocked really hard, hurting his knuckles and making the door rattle against the lock. He could hear the sound echoing through the hall. Then he stepped back from the door and looked along the front of the house. He had not noticed till now that there were shutters up against some of the lower windows. As he looked at them, the holiday feeling went away.

He went back to the door, and rapped on it again, but he knew the house was empty. He tried the latch, but the door was locked. He stood looking at the door.

All right, there it is, he thought. It's been a nice ride. You've had a nice drive in the car. The house is shut up and she has gone away somewhere. That is why the snow in the lane is so flattened down with wheel marks. There's been some comings and goings. She knew all the time that she meant to go away somewhere, and she just told you otherwise to fool you. She gets a kick out of kidding along. She did it in a lot of ways and one too many. All right, this lets you out all right. Your mind has been playing the fool on you ever since you saw her, but this lets you out and it's a good job. When you were cooled off you never wanted to come back to see her again, you only came because you said you would. You were sorry for her and you lied to her when you said it wasn't pity. So this is a bit of luck now. It lets you out and you've enjoyed the drive. What a fool you would have felt if she had been here. What a fool you would have felt.

Then the first thing he knew was a thudding, searing pain across the knuckles of his hand. He drew his clenched fist back from the wooden panel of the door. It was bruised and grazed and starting to bleed, and he bit his teeth together because of the pain, and leaned over to where there was a patch of clean snow at the side of the path, and plunged his fist into it and then rubbed the snow across his knuckles to clean the graze and to freeze the pain. And what did you have to do that for? he asked himself. What in the name of everything did you have to do that for? Did you suddenly go nuts? Did you suddenly stop knowing what your own hand was doing? You'd better watch your temper and you'd better watch that fist of yours. It might not be a door next time. Smashing your fist at a door like that, you're like a spoilt baby.

He gripped his hand tightly round the wrist, to squeeze the pain out. Me and her, he was thinking. Me and her. Me and her.

"You're being a fool!" he said aloud. In the past three weeks he had tried to tell himself a thousand times. What is the matter with you? Do you want to chase around after a painting? Do you want to chase a painting in a magazine?

All right, all right, she showed you something, she did something to you, but now forget it. It was only a silly nothing, a silly nothing in your mind, and it couldn't last long and you ought to have grown out of that kind of feeling. That's all it was, a kind of feeling. It couldn't last long and why doesn't it go away yet? It's a silly nothing and it isn't real. You don't want to waste your time with a thing that isn't real. It's simply a kind of feeling, and yet it doesn't seem to go away. It's a kind of feeling as if she lifts you up to places where you could not reach alone.

And all the time, for ages now, you've been heading for the lonely places. Without this, I mean. For a long time now, you have had a feeling of heading for the lonely places. And now, if you miss this, if you pass this up, if you let this slide, if you turn your back on this, you'll be heading for the lonely places all over again.

With her, he thought, with her there wouldn't ever be any lonely places.

He turned his back on the door of the farmhouse, and started to walk very slowly back along the path. What fun you do think of! he nagged himself. What endless fun you think of picking for yourself. You and a blind girl having fun. The two of you having fun and only one of you being able to have it. You taking your girl to the cinema. "I'll tell you what's happening, darling. The hero has just caught the heroine's eye, now he is walking towards her, now he is raising his hat, she won't speak to him, she's turning her back on him . . . now the scene's changed to a restaurant . . . they're laughing because the funny man has fallen over . . . they're on a train now . . . it keeps showing the wheels whizzing round as if there's going to be an accident . . . the people were gasping then because one of the wheels is loose . . . " oh, shut up, shut up, shut up, he told himself. You don't have to go to the cinema and you're just playing hell with yourself.

He came to the end of the path, to where his car was, and he opened the door and kicked the snow and slush off his shoes against the running-board, and sat in at the wheel. Me and her, he thought. Beside me in the car, now. Me and her. It was no good trying to dodge his thoughts, they clamoured to come at him. Me and her. Someone to whom you could talk the things that are deep inside you. Someone to whom you could talk at last. Someone to share the things that get so heavy when you carry them alone. Me and her, and never any lonely places.

He pressed the starter button, and with his foot on the clutch pedal he turned and looked for another moment at the farmhouse. This is your let-out, he was trying to tell himself. You'll thank your lucky stars about this in a week or two, in a day or two. What did you want with her? What could you ever have wanted with her? You just went soft and queer for a few hours, that's all. James Wilson and a blind girl. Book now for next week's special attraction, James Wilson taking holy orders. Coming shortly, James Wilson fasting in a cage, wearing a hair shirt.

He let the clutch pedal come back slowly as he turned the wheel and sloped the car across the narrow lane. You think of yourself all right, don't you, eh? he asked. It's little you that gets the consideration. It's what you would be missing, that's what counts with you. It isn't what she would be missing that seems to be giving you very much trouble. It is when you think one-sided like that, that is when you are asking for a ticket to those lonely places. You and blessed little stinking you and your hair shirts. You with a feather on your shoulder, trying to paint it to look like a cross. What is it, then? Come on, what is it? If you think of it the other way, then it's pity, and she did not want that. She asked you not to do that. And she didn't have to ask, either, because you have no intention of doing any of that. You can do it to other people, but not to her. Why not? You know why not all right. Because pity makes a substitute for something else, and you'd rather have the something else. You don't want any substitutes for the things you were feeling. You could feel those things all right and you can take them or leave them but you don't want to muck them about.

He put the gear into reverse and backed the car round. You never did want to come back, he told himself. It was only that you promised. You said you would and you didn't like to back out. If she had been here it would just have been a quick hullo and goodbye again, with both of you embarrassed and wishing you had not come. It's lucky you didn't get here before she went away. You wouldn't have known what to say to her, anyway. Your talking practice has been with the smart girls who know the double answers. You wouldn't have known what to say to her.

He started to drive very slowly back along the lane towards the road. So now you can go back. It has been a nice drive, and this is your let-out. Now you can go back to the stinking world in which you live your life. And the lonely places.

He came to the end of the lane, and hesitated which way to turn. Away to the left he could see a small cottage by the side of the road. There was smoke coming out of the chimney. He turned his car that way and stopped outside the cottage. He got out of the car and walked to the door of the cottage and tapped on it. He heard a shuffling inside, and then the door was pulled open by an old man. The old man was wearing a hat, and he touched it politely.

James Wilson pointed in the direction of the farmhouse.

"Did you know Miss Maldon who lived at the farmhouse there?"

"Mary Maldon?"

"Yes."

The old man was affronted at being asked if he knew her. He drew himself up and seemed to gain a couple of inches.

"I've well-nigh run her place for her these last two years," he said.

"Then you'll know where she has gone to now," said James Wilson. He felt something give a little kick inside him.

"I've been like a father to her," the man said, "and she's been like a daughter to me." He spoke slowly and deliberately. It did not seem right to him that someone should ask whether he knew Mary Maldon, and he wanted to deal quite definitely with this piece of ignorance.

"Do you know where she has gone now? I've just been up to the farmhouse, and there's no one there."

"I know there's nobody there." The man was bridling again at the fact that someone was telling him things that were his to know first.

"Do you know where she has gone, then?"

The old man peered very closely at James Wilson.

"Why?" he asked.

"I'm looking for her, that's why."

"You're a stranger round here, aren't you?"

"Yes."

"I thought I hadn't seen you round here before."

"Do you know where she has gone? I'm asking you where Mary Maldon has gone."

"If you're a stranger, then it's none of my business to tell you."

"What do you mean? I'm looking for her, and you're going to tell me where she has gone."

"It's no good your starting to shout at me. I'll tell what I choose, and I won't tell what I don't choose."

"I wasn't shouting at you. I'm only asking where she has gone."

"Well, you're a stranger, and it's none of my business to tell you anything."

"Why not?"

"There were strangers along at her place three weeks ago. Nobody seems to be telling what happened, not even Mary Maldon wouldn't tell me what happened, but I do know as there were strangers along there when her brother killed himself falling up on the hill. The strangers had been up on the hill too, so they must have had something to do with it somehow or other. Everybody round here loves Mary Maldon, and we don't want any strangers bringing her any more trouble. They've brought her enough already."

"But I'm not a stranger to her. I know her."

"You're a stranger to me. You're a stranger in these parts."

"You're just being obstinate and ridiculous. Where has she gone?"

"It's no use you shouting at me. I don't have people shouting at me."

"I'm not shouting at you!"

"Oh, yes, you are, young man. And it isn't going to get you nowhere."

"I want to know where she's gone!"

"Shouting and clenching your fists like that—who do you think you are? Be off with you!" Then the old man vanished abruptly behind the door that was slammed in James Wilson's face.

James Wilson glared at the door, and then turned and went back to his car. What did you want to behave like that for? he wondered. You were curt and shouting enough to put anyone's back up. You could have wheedled it out of him easy as anything, if you hadn't lost your temper. You've coaxed enough things out of enough people in your time. You know how to do it, and it's not like you to let your temper get in your way. What's eating into you so hard? Cut it out, cut it out. You're behaving like a schoolboy. And what over? You don't really care where she has gone, you're just being petulant about it, you just don't like someone stealing a march on James know-all cleversticks Wilson. You've driven all the way up from London, and you feel a little hurt that you didn't find her waiting on her knees for you. You were doing her such a favour by coming to see her again, is that it? You wanted thanks, and you haven't got them. So you stamp and shout and sulk. Well, you'd better be heading for home now. You are glad that you didn't find her. Right inside you, you're glad. Admit that.

He got into his car and sat fingering the wheel indecisively. Ahead of him, further along the road, was the village. There was bound to be someone in the village who at least had some idea as to where she had gone. It could not be difficult to find a clue. He had spent a good many years of his life digging up the tracks of people. This would be easy. He knew that if he turned back now because he could not find her, he would only be lying to himself.

But if you follow her, he thought, if you search her out and follow her, that is very different from just coming back to see her at the farmhouse. It's more pointed. Do you really want to go that far? You have come all the way from London to here, and that was quite enough. Now you find she has gone, and if you go searching her out and chasing after her, then you'll be pushing the nonsense a bit too far. And what would you be chasing, anyway? You'd be like chasing a painting, and you'd be sure to find that the colours did not look so good in a different light.

He sat there in his car, fiddling with the wheel. So when it comes to something, he thought, when it really comes to something, you haven't got the guts to make a clean decision. You don't mind things so long as they follow by easy stages. But when there is a definite fork in the stream, you haven't got the strength inside you to steer your own life. You are ready to float, but you don't want to do any strong swimming. You like to have things feel as if they are happening for you, instead of you making them. Then you can wriggle out of it by blaming fate. It was easy in the farmhouse with her. It all just seemed to float along. And it was easy coming up here again, it did not seem like any big decision. But when it comes to making your mind up, sharply, left or right, then you dally about and dig around for all the excuses you can find. What you deserve is to live the rest of your life in the half-baked, shoddy way you have lived it for the past too many years. You hate it, but it floats along and you don't have to swim.

He pressed the starter button of his car and eased the gear in. All right, he told himself, thanks for the little lecture, but it doesn't seem to fit. Because you made your mind up clear enough, the very first minute. When you saw the shutters at the farmhouse. You knew then, and you still know, that where you want to live is in a real live world with no silly paintings and no hair shirts. *And the next time you let that hair shirt business come into your mind, I'll call you a bastard and I'll really mean it.*

He started to drive very slowly along towards the village. Just out of interest, it might be amusing to see if there was any news to be picked up in the village. Not for doing anything about it, but just out of interest because he had come so far.

He drove slowly through the small village, looking for the post office. It was just a cottage with a letter-box in the wall. He stopped his car and went inside. There was a little wooden counter, and a telephone cubicle. A middle-aged woman came out through a door behind when he rapped on the counter.

"Good afternoon," he said. "I am looking for Miss Mary Maldon. Can you tell me where I can find her?"

"She lives at the farmhouse just off the road about a mile down."

"Yes, I know. But the house seems to be shut up, and I wondered if you knew where she had gone."

"She didn't leave any address here."

"But I thought you might have heard where she'd gone."

"No."

"Do you know how long it is since she went away?"

"About a fortnight."

"Did she go with someone in the village?"

"No. Somebody came to fetch her in a car. They say it was an aunt of hers. I don't know. I daresay that's what she phoned about."

"What who phoned about?"

"Mary Maldon."

"Did she come here to phone?"

"Yes. Old Mr. Harris brought her along here in the trap."

"Where did she phone to?"

"She had a trunk call."

"Don't you remember where it was to?"

"I remember all right. I got the number for her."

"Where was it to?"

"It was to Bradford."

"Bradford? Do you remember the number?"

"No, I don't remember the number. But I know it was to Bradford. I think there was a seven in it."

James Wilson smiled at her.

"Thank you very much," he said. "You've been very kind and very helpful."

He walked out of the post office into the road. That was all he would have needed, if he had wanted anything. The one word, Bradford. That would have been plenty. The call would have been easy enough to trace, and everything else could have been pieced on from there. It was right in his line, that was. You could do it from this end, or you could trace it from the Bradford end. The Bradford end would be better, because then you would be on the spot for the next move. That one word was all he would have needed, if he had wanted anything. If.

He got into his car, and sat there outside the post office. All right, he thought, you can now turn round and go back. There's nothing to stop you. This is your car, and these are your hands on the wheel. You are king of this little petrol-driven castle. You can point it where you like. Tonight you can sleep a hundred miles north, south, east or west. You've all the world to go to. If you want to go and call on someone you can choose from all the people in the world. Yes, you can, and that's the worst of it. You've had all the world to go to before now. You've always had it. And you've been so very good at picking the lonely places. You watch those hands of yours on that wheel of yours. Watch them, keep an eye on them. They are too damned good at taking you to the lonely places.

He got out of the car again, and started to walk slowly along the path through the village. The path had been swept clean of the snow, so that here he could walk without slipping or slushing. He walked slowly, with his eyes on the ground, wriggling with himself, because now another thing was nudging at him, asking to be listened to. It had tried to come before many times, and he had edged it away. Now it was trying with more insistence, and still he was trying to keep it away, but he knew he was losing, he knew that he was going to have to admit this thing that clamoured at the fringes of his mind. You cannot do with dreams forever, he reminded himself. Even if you decided that you wanted to, you still couldn't. You have to face things. Surely it is all right to be material for a bit, isn't it? Strictly material, that is. I mean getting right down to it. It is all very well to keep your mind on other things, but you are human. A man and a woman cannot wholly depend on the mind and the heart. Not only. Not all the time. The mind and the heart alone do not make completeness.

And what about that, with her not seeing? Is it possible to imagine?

Don't try, he wriggled. Stop yourself. Don't be rotten. Don't lower everything. Don't think of her as just a woman. Think of her as Mary.

But he knew that it was not lowering anything really, and that if anything was wrong it was in not facing it, in trying to hide it from himself.

All right, then. What about it? Would it be a kind of inhibited thing? Would it be impossible for it to happen gaily, as it should happen? Would it lack the impromptu lightness of heart that was really the everything of it? Would it just have to be solemn and staid and deliberate, with no little messages beforehand? Would it have to be a plot, a cold decision, at ten-thirty p.m. instead of something that came suddenly springing out of laughter and happiness? Would there be a tune playing in their ears, or only the sounds of the room?

He was thinking about it now, as he walked along the path. And as he walked, and thought of her, his thoughts took hold of him and he suddenly knew the real and uncontradictable truth. And he stopped, and stood still, closing his eyes, knowing that his doubts had been caused by nothing but his own fighting of the thoughts. He knew now that her blindness in that respect was nothing. It meant nothing more than having the lights out in the room. And he knew, from what he already knew, that the tune would be playing and the laughter would be there.

He turned on the path and started back towards his car. The doctors might do something. They had thought they might do something. They would not have said that if they had not got some reason. "Please," he muttered, "please let them do something. Please let them be able to do something for her." It must not matter what it costs, he thought, I would pay every penny I have.

Me and her, he thought. Me and her, and all those things I could not reach alone.

He came to his car again and reached into the cubbyhole of the car and pulled out a road map. He put his finger on Bradford, and then ran his finger along the road between there and where he was, memorising the key places in between. Then he pressed the starter button, and put the gear in, and as the car splashed forward through the melting snow, he could feel again the smile that he did not try to put there.

THE END

FILM NOIR CLASSICS

THE PITFALL Jay Dratler
"Dratler's novel is darker, sleazier and less forgiving than the film it inspired. A brutal portrait of blind lust and self-destruction... a stellar example of 1940s American noir." —Cullen Gallagher, *Pulp Serenade*. Filmed in 1948 with Dick Powell, Lizabeth Scott, Jane Wyatt and Raymond Burr.

FALLEN ANGEL Marty Holland
"This story, about a small-time grifter who lands in a central California town and hooks up with a femme fatale, is straight out of the James M. Cain playbook."—Bill Ott, *Booklist*. Filmed in 1945 with Dana Andrews, Alice Faye and Linda Darnell.

THE VELVET FLEECE
Lois Eby & John C. Fleming
"We guarantee your head will be spinning with double-crosses and you'll be talking out of both sides of your mouth before you finish...." —*Evening Star*.
Filmed as *Larceny* in 1948 starring John Payne, Joan Caulfield and Dan Duryea.

SUDDEN FEAR Edna Sherry
"This is a thoroughly exciting read, with brilliant pacing, which makes you absolutely desperate to know how everything will pan out."—Kate Jackson. Filmed in 1952 with Joan Crawford, Jack Palance and Gloria Grahame.

HOLLOW TRIUMPH Murray Forbes
"...a disturbed personality done in the noir tradition... an atmospheric and evocative yarn that spans the late 30s to through

WWII."—Amazon reader. Filmed in 1948 with Paul Henreid and Joan Bennett as *The Scar*.

THE DARK CORNER /
SLEEP, MY LOVE Leo Rosten
"The slang is tangy, the plots magnetic, the suspense sweet, the hilarity edgy... For all lovers of vintage noir."
—Donna Seaman, *Booklist*. Filmed in 1946 and 1948 with Lucille Ball, Clifton Well, Claudette Colbert and Robert Cummings.

DEADLIER THAN THE MALE
James Gunn
"The attitude of the book... reels between black comedy and surrealism drenched in a misanthropy that is occasionally stunning."—Ed Gorman. Filmed as *Born to Kill* in 1947 with Lawrence Tierney and Claire Trevor.

KISS THE BLOOD OFF MY HANDS
Gerald Butler
"The violence, crime, brutality, and 'trapped-in-a-narrow-place' aspects of noir are all here."—Carl Waluconis. Filmed in 1948 with Joan Fontaine and Burt Lancaster.

MOONRISE Theodore Strauss
"Moonrise is unique in that it's one of the few noirs in which the redemptive power of love holds nihilism at bay."—Eddie Muller. Filmed in 1948 with Dane Clark and Gail Russell.

In trade paperback from...
Stark House Press, 1315 H Street, Eureka, CA 95501
greg@starkhousepress.com / www.StarkHousePress.com
Available from your local bookstore, or order direct via our website.

www.ingramcontent.com/pod-product-compliance
Lightning Source LLC
Chambersburg PA
CBHW050343160726
48002CB00001B/441